Moy McCrory

was born in Liverpool and educ[...]
lives in Salisbury.

By the same author

THE WATER'S EDGE
BLEEDING SINNERS
THE FADING SHRINE

MOY McCRORY

Those Sailing Ships of His Boyhood Dreams

Flamingo
An Imprint of HarperCollins*Publishers*

Flamingo
An Imprint of HarperCollins*Publishers*
77–85 Fulham Palace Road,
Hammersmith, London W6 8JB

Published by Flamingo 1992
9 8 7 6 5 4 3 2 1

First published in Great Britain by
Jonathan Cape 1991

Copyright © Moy McCrory 1991

The Author asserts the moral right to
be identified as the author of this work

'The Wrong Vocation' previously appeared in the
Critical Quarterly and *Best British Stories*; 'Nancy and the
Last Ever Monkey' was broadcast by BBC Radio Four
and Radio Five; 'The O'Tourney Sisters and the
Day of Reckoning' first appeared in the *Irish Times*.

ISBN 0 00 654439 8

Set in Meridien

Printed in Great Britain by
HarperCollinsManufacturing Glasgow

All rights reserved. No part of this publication may be
reproduced, stored in a retrieval system, or transmitted,
in any form or by any means, electronic, mechanical,
photocopying, recording or otherwise, without the prior
permission of the publishers.

This book is sold subject to the condition that it shall not,
by way of trade or otherwise, be lent, re-sold, hired out or
otherwise circulated without the publisher's prior consent
in any form of binding or cover other than that in which it
is published and without a similar condition including this
condition being imposed on the subsequent purchaser.

Contents

The Wrong Vocation	1
Ruby's Big Night	15
Nancy and the Last Ever Monkey	29
Maeve the Broken-hearted	37
Three Views From a House	47
The O'Touney Sisters and the Day of Reckoning	61
The Mermaid and the Rat Catcher	73
Eiffel Tower	83
The Faithful Departed	101
Burn Bright Those Yuletide Logs	117
A Fine Voice You Have Ma'am	127
A Well Travelled Woman	133
Those Sailing Ships of His Boyhood Dreams	147

The Wrong Vocation

'When God calls you, he is never denied' Sister Mercy told us with a finality which struck terror into our hearts.

She stood at the front of the room with the window behind her, so we were blinded and could not see her features but we knew she smiled.

'He waits patiently until we hear his voice. When that happens, you are never the same.'

It terrified me that this thing called a vocation might come dropping in to my mind out of nowhere one day and wedge there like a piece of grit.

'God is looking now, seeing who is pure of heart and ready to be offered up.'

Every girl shifted uncomfortably. Sister looked at our upturned faces and seemed pleased with the effect she was having. By way of illustration she told us about a young woman from a rich home who was always laughing, with young men waiting to escort her here, there and everywhere, and a big family house with chandeliers in the rooms and a lake in the garden.

'I've seen it. It was on the telly the other night,' Nancy Lyons whispered to me.

'With all these good things in life, she was spoiled. Her wealthy father indulged his daughter's every wish. And do you think she was happy?'

'She damned well ought to be,' Nancy hissed while around us the more pious members of the form shook their heads.

Sister placed her bony hands across her chest and stood up on her tiptoes as if reaching with her rib cage for something that would constantly evade it.

'Her heart was empty.'

Sister went on to tell us how the young woman resisted the call, but eventually realised she would never be happy until she

Those Sailing Ships of His Boyhood Dreams

devoted her life to Christ. Going out beside the lake, she asked him to enter her life.

'She is one of our very own nuns, right here in this convent. Of course I cannot tell you which sister she is, but when you imagine that we were all born as nuns, remember that we were once young girls like yourselves, without a thought in our heads that we should devote our lives to God.'

There was a silence. We all stared out past her head.

'Oh, Sister, it's beautiful,' said a voice. Nancy rolled her eyes to heaven. Lumpy, boring Beatrice who always sat at the front would like it. She was so slow-witted and so good. She was one of the least popular girls in the class, a reporter of bad news and always the first to give homework in. With mini skirts de rigueur, her uniform remained stoically unadapted. She must have been the only girl in the school that did not need to have her hemline checked at the end of the day. While we struggled to turn over our waistbands Beatrice always wore her skirt a good two inches below her plump knees and looked like one of the early photographs, all sepia and foggy, of the old girls in their heyday.

Nancy pulled a face.

'But wasn't her rich father angry?' someone asked, and Sister Mercy nodded.

'Mine would sodding kill me. They don't even want me to stay on at school. Me mother's always reminding me how much money they're losing because I'm not bringing any wages home.'

'Do you have something to say, Nancy Lyons?' Sister's stern voice rapped.

'No Sister, I was just saying what a great sacrifice it was to make.'

'Ah yes, a great sacrifice indeed.'

But the sacrifice was not just on the nun's part. Everyone else was made to suffer. There was a woman in our street who never recovered after her eldest daughter joined the Carmelites. Mrs Roddy's daughter was a teacher in the order. It was not the fact that she would never give her mother grandchildren that caused the greatest upset, but the economics of it. All a nun's earnings go straight back into the convent. Mrs Roddy used to wring her hands.

'That money's mine,' she would shout, 'for feeding and clothing her all those years. The church has no right to it!'

Then her daughter went peculiar. We only noticed because they sent her home for a week on holiday, and we thought that was unusual, but it was around the time they were relaxing the rule. Nuns were appearing on the streets with skirts that let them walk easily, skimming their calves instead of the pavement.

During that week she got her cousin to perm her hair, on account of the new headdress. She assured her that it was all right because even nuns had to look groomed now their hair showed at the front, and every night she continued to lead the family in the joyful mysteries.

'I'll tell you Mrs Mac, I'm worn out with all the praying since our Delcia's been back,' her mother would confide to mine as they passed quickly in the street, while her daughter muttered 'God bless you' to no one in particular and with a vague smile.

But indoors, she borrowed her mother's lipstick, deep red because Mrs Roddy still had the same one from before the war. That was when they thought she was going a bit far, when they saw her outmoded, crimson mouth chanting the rosary. She drove her family mad. She had tantrums and kept slamming doors. Then they saw her out in the street asking to be taken for rides on Nessie Moran's motorbike. Everyone said she had taken her vows too young. She crammed all those teenage things she never did into that week. By the end of it they were relieved to send her back.

Her mother hated nuns. She did not mind priests half as much.

'At least they're human' she would say. 'Well, half human. Nuns aren't people. They're not proper women. They don't know what it is to be a mother and they'll never be high up in the church. They'll never be the next pope. They can't even say mass. What good are they? They're stuck in the middle, not one thing or the other. Brides of Christ! They made me sick. Let them try cooking, cleaning and running a home on nothing. I'd have a damned easier life if I'd married Christ, instead of that lazy bugger inside.'

But she was fond of the young priest at her church, a good looking, fresh faced man from Antrim who would sit and have a drink with them at the parish club.

Those Sailing Ships of His Boyhood Dreams

'At least you can have a laugh with him,' she'd say, 'but that stuck up lot, they're all po-faced up at Saint Ursula's. They're no better than any of us. I'm a woman, don't I know what their minds are like. They're no different. Gossipy, unnatural creatures, those ones are. Look what's happened to our poor Delcia after being with them.'

And then the convent sent Delcia home to be looked after by her family. An extended holiday they called it, on account of her stress and exhaustion.

'They've used her up, now they don't want what's left over, so I've got her again. What good is she to anyone now? She can't look after herself. She can't even make a bloody cup of tea. How will she fend for herself if the order won't have her back? I'm dying, Mrs Mac, I can't be doing with her.'

My mother would tut and nod and shut the door.

'It's a shame. What sort of a life has that poor girl had?' she would say indoors, shaking her head at the tragedy.

'I know she's gone soft now, but she was good at school. Her mam and dad thought she'd be something and now she's fit for nothing if the church can't keep her.'

In the evening we would hear Mrs Roddy shouting 'Get in off the street!'

Finally they took her into a hospice and we heard no more about it, but Mrs Roddy always crossed the road to avoid nuns. Once outside Lewis's a Poor Clare thrust a collection box at her and asked for a donation. Mrs Roddy tried to take it from her and the box was pulled back and forth like a bird tugging at a worm. It was not the nun's iron grip, but the bit of elastic which wrapped itself around her wrist that foiled Mrs Roddy's attempt to redistribute the church's wealth.

'They're just like vultures,' she would say, 'waiting to see what they can tear from your limbs. They're only happy when they've picked you clean. Better hide your purses!'

At the collection on Sundays she sat tight lipped and the servers knew better than to pass the collecting plate her way.

'A vocation gone wrong,' was what my father called Delcia Roddy. He would shake his head from side to side and murmur things like 'the shame' or 'the waste'. He had a great deal of sympathy for her tortured soul. It was about this time that I became tortured. He had none for me.

Sister Mercy's words had stung like gravel in a grazed knee. At night I could hear them as her voice insisted, 'You cannot fight God's plan,' and I would pray that God keep his plans to himself.

'You must pray for a vocation,' she told us.

I gritted my teeth and begged His Blessed Mother to intervene.

'I'll be worse than the Roddy girl,' I threatened, 'and look what a disgrace she was.' Then, echoing the epitaph of W. B. Yeats, I would point into the darkness and urge 'Horseman; Pass by!'

'We are instruments of God's will,' Sister Mercy told us and I did not want to be an instrument.

I knew if God had any sense he would not want me, but Sister Mercy frightened us. Beatrice was the one headed for a convent. She had made plain her intentions at the last retreat when she stood up and announced to the study group that she was thinking of devoting her life to Christ.

'She may as well, there's nothing else down for her,' Nancy commented.

Yet Sister Mercy told us that often the ones we did not suspect had vocations, and she looked around the room like a mind-reader scrutinising the audience before pulling out likely candidates.

The convent terrified me; the vocation stalked my shadow like a store detective. One day it would pounce and I would be deadlocked into a religious life, my will subsumed by one greater than I. Up there was a rapacious appetite which consumed whole lives, like chicken legs. I dreaded that I should end up in a place where every day promised the same, the gates locked behind me and all other escape sealed off. It wasn't that I had any ambitions for what I might do, but I could not happily reconcile myself to an existence where the main attraction was death. I dreaded hearing God's call.

'He can wait for years. God is patient.'

I decided that I would have to exasperate him, and fast.

Down at the Pier Head, pigeons gathered in thousands. The Liver Buildings were obscured as they all rose in unison like a blanket of grey and down. I never knew where my fear came from, but I was terrified of those birds. Harmless seagulls twice their size flew about me, followed the ferry out across the water to Birkenhead and landed flapping and breathless on the landing plank. Their screech was piercing. They never disturbed me. Yet when I stepped out into Hamilton Square and saw the tiny cluster of city birds waiting, my heart would beat in panic. City birds who left slime where they went, their excrement the colour of the new granite buildings springing up. They nodded their heads and watched you out of the corners of their eyes. They knocked smaller birds out of the way and I had seen them taking bread away from each other. They were a fighting, quarrelsome brood, an untidy shambling army, with nothing to do all day but walk around the Pier Head or follow me through Princess Park and make my life a misery.

Once I was crossing for a bus, just as a streak of them flew up into the air. I put my hands over my head, the worst fear being that one should touch my face, and I could think of nothing more sickening than the feel of one of these ragged creatures, bloated with disease, the flying vermin which flocked around the Life Assurance building, to remind us we were mortal.

I had a nightmare at the time of being buried alive under thousands of these birds. They would make that strange cooing noise as they slowly suffocated me. Their fat greasy bodies would pulsate and swell, as satiated, they nestled down onto me for the heat my body could provide. Under this sweltering, stinking mass I would be unable to scream. Each time I opened my mouth it filled with dusty feathers.

They my nightmare changed. Another element crept into my dreams. Alongside the pigeons crept the awful shape that was a vocation. It came in all colours, brown and white, black and white, beige, mottled, grey and sandy, as the different robes of each order clustered around me, knocking pigeons out of the way. They muttered snatches of Latin, bits of psalms, and rubbed their clawed hands together like banktellers. The big change in the dream was that they, unlike the pigeons, did not suffocate me, but slowly drew away, leaving me alone in a great empty space, which at first I thought was the bus terminal, but which Nancy Lyons assured me was the image of my life to be.

The Wrong Vocation

Her older sister read tea leaves and was very interested in dreams. Nancy borrowed a book from her.

'It says here, that dreaming about water means a birth.'

'I was dreaming about pigeons, and then nuns.'

'Yeah, but you said you were down at the Pier Head didn't you, and that's water.'

'I don't know if I was at the Pier Head.'

'Oh you must have been. Where else would you get all them pigeons?' Nancy was a realist.' Water means a birth,' she repeated firmly. 'I bet your mam gets pregnant.'

I knew she was wrong. I was the last my mother would ever have, she told me often enough. But Nancy would not be put off. The book was lacking on nuns so she held out for the water and maintained that the big empty space was my future.

'There's nothing down for you unless you go with the sisters,' she said.

It was not because I lacked faith that I dreaded the vocation. I suffered from its excesses, it hung around me, watching every move, and passing judgement. I was a failed miserable sinner and I knew it, but I did not want to atone. I did not want the empty future I was sure it offered. Our interpretation of the dream differed.

Around this time I had a Saturday job in a delicatessen in town. I was on the cold-meat counter. None of the girls were allowed to touch the bacon slicer. Only Mister Calderbraith could do that. He wore a white coat and must have fancied himself as an engineer the way he carried on about the gauge of the blades. He would spend hours unscrewing the metal plates and cleaning out the bolts and screws with a look of extreme concentration on his face.

His balding head put out a few dark strands of hair which he grew to a ludicrous length and wore combed across his scalp to give the impression of growth. Some of the girls said he wore a toupee after work, and that if we were to meet him on a Sunday we would not know him.

He used to pretend he was the manager. He would come over and ask customers solicitously if everything was all right and remark that if the service was slow, it was because he was breaking in new staff.

Those Sailing Ships of His Boyhood Dreams

'Who does he think he's kidding!' Elsie said after he had leaned across the counter one morning. 'He couldn't break in his shoes.'

Shoes were a problem. I was on my feet all day, and they would ache by the time we came to cash up. I used to catch the bus from the Pier Head at around five-thirty, if I could get the glass of the counter wiped down and the till cashed. The manager and seniors were obsessed with dishonesty. Cashing up had to be done in strict military formation. None of us were allowed to move until we heard a bell and the assistant manager would take the cash floats from us in silence.

Inside his glass office the manager sat on a high stool with mirrors all around him, surveying us. If any of the girls sneezed, or moved out of synch another bell would sound and we would all have to instantly shut our tills while the manager shouted over the loudspeaker system, 'Disturbance at counter number four' or wherever it was. Sometimes it took ages.

They never failed to inform us that staff were all dishonest. Not the management, Mister Calderbraith or senior staff, but the floor workers, and especially the temporary staff, the Saturday workers, because as they told us, we had the least to lose, and we were 'fly by nights' according to the manager, who grinned as he told us that.

I could not imagine anything there worth stealing. It was all continental meats and strange cheeses that smelt strongly, the mouldier the better.

'Have you seen that bread they're selling?' Elsie said to me one Saturday.

'The stuff that looks like it's got mouse droppings on top?'

But people came from all over the city and placed orders.

One Saturday evening I was waiting for the next bus having missed the five-thirty. My feet ached. The manager would not let you sit down. Even when there were no customers in sight you were supposed to stand to attention. I took it in turns with Elsie to duck beneath the wooden counter supports and sit on the floor when business was slack. Whenever Mister Calderbraith was about, we both stood rigidly. He loathed serving customers.

'See to that lady,' he would say if anyone asked him for a quarter of liver sausage.

The Wrong Vocation

I had worn the wrong shoes, they had heels. Throughout the week I wore comfortable brown lace-ups, but at the weekend I wanted to wear things that did not scream 'schoolgirl'. But my mother had been right. I was crippled.

After a few minutes I leant back on the rail and kicked one shoe off. My toes looked puffy and red. I put that one back and kicked off the other. It shot into the gutter. Before I had a chance to hop after it, a pigeon the size of a cat flapped down and stood between it and me. It looked at me, then slowly began to walk around the shoe. I was rigid, gripping the rail and keeping my foot off the pavement. Then the bird hopped inside the shoe and seemed to settle as a hen might in a nest. It began to coo. I was perspiring. I would never be able to take the shoe from it, and even if I managed to I would not be able to put my foot inside after that vile creature had sat in it. I was desperate. Suddenly, as if it sensed my fright, it flew up in the air towards me almost brushing my face with its wings, then it circled and landed squarely back inside the shoe. I did not wait. It could have it. I hopped away from the bus stop and limped towards the taxi stand. I reckoned I had just enough money to get a cab home. It would be all my pay for the Saturday, and I would not be able to go out that night, but I did not care. It would take me, shoeless, right to the front door and away from the pigeon.

Then, I thought it was my mind playing tricks, but I saw three shapes blowing in the breeze, veils flapping behind them. The Pier Head was so windy, I thought they might become airborne. They got bigger and bigger. I was certain that they flew. Soon they would be right on top of me. God was giving me a sign. The Vocation had decided to swoop after so long pecking into my dreams. Three silent figures, as mysterious as the Trinity, crossed the tarmac of the bus terminal. I could not take my eyes from them. They seemed to swell the way a pigeon puffs out its chest to make itself important. They were getting fatter and rounder like brown and white balloons. Carmelites. I could not stay where I was. I had to escape. Some people moved to one side as I hobbled to a grass verge. I tripped on the concrete rim of the grassy area and caught my ankle. As I put my hand down to catch myself, several birds pecking on rubbish, rose into the air just in front of me, and I thought for one deluded second that I was flying with

Those Sailing Ships of His Boyhood Dreams

them as the white sky span and I tumbled over. Only when my head came level with a brown paper carrier bag did I smell the grossly familiar scent of cold meats.

'Young lady, are you in some sort of difficulty?'

The voice of Mister Calderbraith pulled me out of my terrified stupor. I lifted my head and came eye to quizzical eye.

'Whatever is wrong with you? Can't you walk properly? Good heavens, what has happened to your shoe? Have you been in some sort of incident?' He straightened up and looked around desperately.

'Tell me who did it,' he insisted. 'Check that you still have your front door keys.'

I raised myself up on one knee and obediently opened my bag. Everything was intact. Mister Calderbraith's eyes opened wide.

'I really don't understand . . .' he began.

Behind him I could see a triangle formation moving against the empty sky. The three sisters seemed to glide inside its rigid outline like characters in the medals people brought back from Fatima. Behind them flapped wings, veils, patches of brown, and feathers. Dark against the white sky they enveloped me, just as my dream had forewarned. I could not speak. My hands shook.

'What is it? Have you seen the culprit?'

I nodded, still struggling to rise.

'They often work in a gang, these hoodlums,' Mister Calderbraith continued. 'Oh, yes. I've watched enough detective programmes to know how they operate.' He glanced from side to side furtively.

'They've probably left their lookout nearby. Acting casual.' He glowered menacingly at the passers-by.

They were closing in behind Mister Calderbraith. They peered over his shoulder. Inhuman they cheeped and shrieked. I could not understand a thing. Mister Calderbraith nodded at me, his head pecking up and down. I reached out and pointed and a dreadful magnetic force pulled me towards them. I was on my feet in seconds.

Mister Calderbraith turned round and saw the three. He shrank away from them.

'You don't mean these, surely?' he said. 'That is stretching it.

Have you been drinking? Tell me, were you on relief at the spirit counter?'

'She's had a bit of a fall,' a passer-by said.

'I think she fell on her head,' Mister Calderbraith nodded.

Then turning to the spectators who had crossed from the bus shelter, he reassured them that everything was all right.

'She is one of my staff members, it's all under control, I know this young lady. Let me deal with it.'

The smallest nun, a tiny frail sparrow, hopped lightly towards me, concern marked by the way she held her head on one side. Her scrawny hand scratched at the ground and she caught up a carrier bag that lay askew on the grass verge. The others clucked solicitously. Then there was a stillness. All fluttering seemed to stop. She handed the bag to me and I took it as my voice returned to tumble out in hopeless apologies while my face burned. Hugging the carrier bag to me, I stumbled towards a taxi which had pulled up. I fell inside and slammed the door. I breathed deeply, thinking that I was going to cry from embarrassment. Out of the back window I could see the nuns standing with Mister Calderbraith who was looking about as if he had lost something.

'Where to, love?' the driver asked.

My voice was thin and wavery as I told him. I put my head back and sighed. Only when we were halfway along the Dock Road did I realise that I was still hugging the bag. I peered inside. It was stuffed with pieces of meat, slivers of pork and ends of joints, all wrapped up in Mr Calderbraith's sandwich papers. There was a great knuckle of honey roast ham. It would be a sin to waste it.

Then I started to laugh. I couldn't stop. Tears ran down my face. Sister Mercy had told us that we had to be spotless, our souls bleached in God's grace. We had to repent our past and ask Him to take up residence in our hearts. I put my hand into the bag and drew out a piece of meat. I crammed it into my mouth. I swallowed my guilt, ate it whole and let it fill by body. As I chewed I wondered at how I still felt the same. I was no different, only now I had become the receiver of stolen goods. I wondered if Mister Calderbraith would be nicer to me? I would not be surprised if he let me have a go on the bacon slicer, next weekend.

'Are you all right love?' the driver asked.

I was choking on a piece of meat.

'I'm fine,' I coughed, scarcely waiting long enough before I stuffed another bit into my mouth. I ate with frenzied gulping sounds. When I looked up I saw the driver watching me in his mirror.

'God, but you must be starving,' he said.

I nodded.

'Well you're a growing girl. You don't know how lucky you are to have all your life in front of you.'

'I do, I really do,' I told him as I pulled another bit of meat off a bone with my teeth. Between mouthfuls I laughed. My one regret was that it wasn't a Friday – I could have doubled my sin then without any effort. Then I realised that I had subverted three nuns into being accomplices. What more did I need?

I slapped my knees and howled. God would have to be desperate to want me now.

As the taxi pulled up outside the house, I saw the curtains twitch. I did not know how I was going to explain losing my shoe, but nothing could lower my spirits, not even hiccups.

Ruby's Big Night

Ruby finished stitching the twenty-fifth fake pearl to the bodice of the gown. Twenty-five a day she had promised herself ever since she had assembled the dress into one piece and hung it under plastic in the wardrobe.

Men had it easy, no doubt about it. One good black suit and it lasted a lifetime. You could be buried in it, if you didn't put on too much weight. She patted her stomach. She was proud of her physique. Always slim, she never had to worry, not like some women. Drive you round the twist with their diets and counting.

Ethel, God rest her, saw everything she ate as a number. At the end of the day she'd sit down and study a list of figures she'd scrawled in a book and pass it to her husband to check the total. She used to buy notebooks and little plastic diaries specially. She was a thorough woman who never threw anything out. After she died they found all her little books in a shoebox on top of the wardrobe. Years and years of lists. Every item of food, every meal Ethel had eaten during thirty-seven years of marriage was entered with its calorific equation. They couldn't believe it. She never looked any different. A fitting epitaph for her would have simply said 'Half a grapefruit – 50'.

Ruby carefully hung the blue dress back in its place of honour. She had removed everything else, except a three-piece suit of Jack's which she could not bear to throw out, and the dress hung freely without being crushed up against the sensible skirts and blouses she always wore.

What would Jack think if he could see her? Ruby was sure that he could and imagined him smiling like an indulgent parent. But her daughter had been terrible. Brian had told her as soon as their father was dead, 'He's gone mam, you've got to carry on without him. Start going out, try to get an interest that takes you outside the house.'

Those Sailing Ships of His Boyhood Dreams

But Mary had taken Jack's death harder. You'd have thought it was her husband, not her father, the way she carried on. Her two little ones were terrified. Never seen mummy cry. She'd never seen Mary cry like that either. Worse than a kid.

She didn't remember her being a whinger, that was left to Brian because he was sickly. Well, they'd both done all right by her and Jack – they'd been reared properly.

The sadness that arrived at unpredictable times caught her then, and she sat weakly on the folorn double bed. I miss you lad, I miss you.

'It's that soddin' house,' Mary had said. 'Everywhere you look there's Dad's things. I keep expecting him to come in and sit down. Any minute now he'll walk back in and watch telly like nothing's changed. As soon as I'm in the door I can smell his shaving soap. You'll have to get rid of his things Mam, otherwise you'll always be trapped. I keep thinking he's in the next room, only as soon as I go in he leaves it. It's like he's avoiding me.'

Ruby didn't tell them that at night when the house was very still she would lie in their bed and listen. Then she would hear his footsteps along the landing. Hear him run the taps in the bathroom and hunt in the hot press for a warm towel. She always left a clean one for him and in the morning she would look for traces, praying to Saint Veronica, but he didn't leave so much as a scum mark. The dead create very little housework.

She wondered if she would finish the dress in time. Why wouldn't she? There were no excuses – she didn't have to stop to cook dinner for anyone, or keep the house tidy, she didn't have to do anyone's washing or iron awkward shirts with temperamental collars that turned the wrong way. No, she didn't have to do anything at all. The day yawned and stretched. Why get out of bed, you only have to come back here at the end of it? Save yourself the effort.

Mary had been good, bringing hot meals round when she saw that she wasn't bothering. But even then she had no appetite for anything. What would she do with herself? This was the golden retirement they had both looked forward to so eagerly. Travel? They had planned routes. But not now, not on her own. She sat further back on the bed and stretched her legs in front so they hung over the edge. The blue dress seemed to wink from the half-open door of the wardrobe.

It was her first proper ballroom frock. Ever since she had joined the Ladies Over Fifties Formation team, they had been hard at work getting their outfits ready. And blue was a lucky choice because it suited her. Some of the others would look like they were dying.

The ballroom dancing had been a chance item one night on T.V. It reminded her of the days before she was married, when she'd loved dancing. In fact she'd met Jack at the Gresham. It was only later that she realised he'd been sitting down. She never saw him dance. Well, at the time she just thought that some men aren't too fond of dancing, and she was never without partners in those days. She was always popular and there were some grand dancers then, not like now.

The young people are all wild. Disco they call it and not a step among them. If you told them the next one was a Valeta they'd look at you soft. But even the big ballrooms have disco interludes now. She always sat them out.

People that had been loafing round all evening would suddenly take to the floor and jump around like cave-men. No breeding. And God, the music would near deafen you. You couldn't speak. She'd shouted herself hoarse trying to get served with a mineral water.

But, back in those days it was real music. That's when she'd noticed Jack. He always hung back from the crowd. He was never brash, never carrying on.

'He likes you,' Ethel told her. Ethel, squeezed into a pink lace frock with the rolls of her stomach pushing through.

'Ten more days on the diet and this'll fit. The shop assistant kept telling me I wanted the next size up, but I told her. "You won't know me in a fortnight," I said. You should have seen her face. Cheeky bitch!'

Ruby remembered the time Jack had shyly asked her if she wanted to see that week's film at the Rio and she'd got all flustered because he wasn't like the others and said yes, although she'd already been to the matinee on Saturday with Ethel.

She got there early and could have kicked herself because he wasn't there. Then she saw him, and that was when she noticed his slow dragging walk, one foot weighed down by a heavy boot, the sole three or four inches thick. And he knew she'd seen it. You can't keep something like that a secret can you, she thought. And he glanced down awkwardly at his cursed foot as if he'd have to introduce it. But she took his arm and acted brighter than she felt because she was embarrassed. And she didn't once look down at the pavement.

She gave up dancing because it didn't seem fair. She couldn't be out with other fellows, and him sitting there looking on. It was no sacrifice. She didn't want him to feel that he wasn't good enough for her on account of his foot. But he had said something not that long before he died. People go a bit funny, start re-living their past, and he'd shock her some days, remembering something she'd long forgotten. That was when he told her that one of the things he'd regretted was that she'd stopped dancing. He said that he used to love watching her. He said it was because she was proud and graceful, and he had wanted everyone to know that that was his girl out there on the patterned floor, moving to the rhythms of the dance band in their smart lilac jackets.

'I never wanted you to stop, just wanted you to go on dancing for ever and ever those nights. I wanted the band to keep playing into morning, I was that proud of you.'

'Well, I was a lot younger then,' she laughed.

'There was no one your match in those days,' he told her. 'No one. I'd sit listening. They'd ask each other who you were, try to find out your name, and dare themselves to ask you for a dance. I never minded. Hop-along-Jack got to take you home in a taxi at the end of it all. They envied me. They couldn't work it out.'

'You must get an interest outside the house,' her son told her when Jack died.

'Join a club, try something new.' So she enrolled for ballroom dancing.

'What's brought that on?' Mary asked her, shrieking with laughter. 'You've never gone dancing in your life!'

Not in your life I haven't. But Mary couldn't stop laughing. She'd show her. It spurred her on. What started as a pastime took over her life. She had a flair for it they said, and she was invited to join the formation team. Although one of the oldest, she quickly

Ruby's Big Night

became one of their better dancers.

At nights she studied charts with tiny black footprints on; the cha-cha, the rumba, it all came back to her. The charts really confused her but Mrs Eckersby the trainer told her they had gone modern and this was the new teaching method, so Ruby pretended that she had studied them. She persevered and even passed an exam.

The day the certificate came Brian framed it. And what did Mary do? Took one look and had to leave the room. They could hear her trying to control her laughter in the passage way.

'I know it's all a big joke to you,' Ruby yelled, and Mary came back, her eyes still watering and apologised.

But this was it. Competitive dance in the Locarno Ballroom, Scarborough. Oh, Jack, I wish you could be there to sit on the sides and encourage me.

She opened the drawer. Inside lay the gilt edged ticket with 'complimentary pass' stamped in red letters. Next to it was the programme with a special leaflet, 'Notes for Competitors', poking out.

She would be away with the dancing team and Mrs Eckersby for a whole weekend. She counted up. Only three more weeks. She'd have to up the pearls to thirty a day if she was to get it finished.

Scarborough's Locarno Ballroom shimmered. Ruby sat anxiously with the Ladies' team. She sipped her orange squash and hoped she would not have to keep running to the toilet. She took another small mouthful because her lips felt dry, and pushed the glass away from her. They sat in two rows on opposite sides of one long formica table littered with untouched glasses of lemon barley, minerals and cokes.

Mrs Eckersby wouldn't let them drink anything stronger before they went on.

'You're in training, Ladies,' she would remind them. 'No alcohol until you've finished your set. Clear heads and sharp minds are needed for precision formation.' Precision formation, she made it sound so important. And that's what they were, a precision team, split-second timing, turning on a sixpence. It all ran through Ruby's mind, all the practice sessions to get it right, with Mrs Eckersby making them do the same movements over

Those Sailing Ships of His Boyhood Dreams

and over, until they could dance the set in their sleep. They were a team, all for one and one for all, Mrs Eckersby told them. She hoped she wouldn't let them down. Let someone else forget the steps, she prayed. If we have to get it wrong, just don't let it be me.

She noticed there seemed to be some sort of commotion at the furthest end of the table where Mrs Godison was sitting. She'd had a blue rinse put in that afternoon at a hairdresser's along the seafront.

'I couldn't get booked up with my usual girl,' she'd wailed all the way on the coach. 'What'll I do?'

Her hair was stiff, the tips navy blue.

'Look what they've gone and done,' she said when she returned to the hotel. 'Oh, I should never have let that trainee near me.'

Someone's chance comment had started her off again. A team mate laughed, wondering if they'd have green hair under the coloured lights.

'Won't we look funny with pink and blue heads?' she'd grinned, and Mrs Godison began to look upset.

'Is it that bad?' she asked, patting it.

'It will wash out soon enough,' her partner told her, which was the wrong thing to say.

'They knew you were desperate,' someone said.

'They told me it was the only way I'd get an appointment at such short notice.'

'Well I suppose they have to start somewhere don't they? I mean, they have to be let loose on their first customer sometime.'

'Oh, it's not that bad,' Mrs Godison's partner said, but it was too late. The stiff head of hair hung down and beneath the rigid halo could be heard the sound of sobbing.

'Look what you've done now!' Her partner turned to the speaker.

'All I said was they have to start somewhere . . . ' Several of the team nodded in agreement. Mrs Godison had irritated them all morning, asking if anyone knew a good hairdresser in Scarborough and fretting ever since the coach left the bus station. Now her heavy frame wrung out sob after sob.

'Some folks are too sensitive by half. They think everyone's looking at them,' she continued.

Ruby's Big Night

But Mrs Eckersby was on her way down the table.

'Where's your handbag?' she demanded. 'Now wipe your eyes.'

Trust Mrs Eckersby to assess the situation and take control like that.

'Get this down you,' Ruby heard her telling Mrs Godison as a glass of dark brown liquid was passed over from the bar.

The distraught woman sniffed it first then emptied it in one expert movement of her head. She patted her face with a tissue and asked if her face powder was streaky.

'No, you look fine. Just run a comb through your hair.'

Mrs Godison's face crumpled and she lost control for the second time.

'Pull yourself together,' Mrs Eckersby told her. 'You can't let the team down. A chain is only as strong as its weakest link and we all pull together, one for all and all for one,' she said, getting confused as she was forced to start her pep talk earlier than she might have wanted.

Ruby knew she could never do that, encourage them, urge them along and always be ready to deal with incidents. She'd panicked when she'd been elected as the team's first aider, and that was different, that was sprained ankles not emotional upsets. She had been the safety rep years before at work when she was a telephonist. Only because she'd do anything then to get an afternoon away from the switchboard. As soon as the team heard, they asked if she would mind going on a refresher course. So she did. This time she paid special attention to strapping up ankles and putting legs in splints. She was always terrified one of them might slip and put their back out, because she hadn't done backs really. Slipped discs were a bit advanced and the class she went to spent a long time with the kiss of life, much use that would be to her. But when she'd enrolled she'd ticked a box for indoor sports and that included swimming so she spent several evenings bent over a ghastly wax dummy trying to see if she could get two rubber balloons to inflate.

But Mrs Eckersby had insisted.

'We'll be prepared for anything, it's like taking out insurance. Mrs Harper will have us covered,' and she'd smiled at Ruby. She was always very formal. She called all the team members Mrs this and Miss that for any unfortunates.

Those Sailing Ships of His Boyhood Dreams

'We are a professional outfit,' Mrs Eckersby told them, and in the cause of greater professionalism, Ruby took along to every practice the little green first aid box and laid it ceremoniously on the piano in the hall.

'It's these attentions to detail that make us special,' their trainer told them, and they all felt better for seeing the box.

Ruby couldn't get closer to Mrs Godison. She scraped back the tightly packed chairs and leaned in her direction.

'Is she going to be all right?'

'The daft old fool, of course she will be,' a team member snapped. 'She'll get on that dance floor and she won't put a foot wrong. If she does, I'll kill her.'

Around Mrs Godison four team mates were patting her arms and making sympathetic noises. The woman's eyes looked red-rimmed, but she was smiling.

Mrs Eckersby clapped her hands. When she spoke she used her official voice and they knew they were coming up to their time.

'We go on straight after the Northern Colliery Troupe, in the Old Time Sequence section.'

That was it. Mrs Godison's outburst was forgotten as the entire table stood. They walked holding their stomachs in and their chins out as they had been taught.

'Never forget, you are diplomats for Bolton,' Mrs Eckersby reminded them.

The Northern Colliery Troupe were already in position, the wives and partners in pink and yellow, a dreadful combination, and the men stiff in black suits like six undertakers. Out on the ballroom floor the exhibition team had the audience mesmerised.

'We'd never manage that,' someone said as the team performed a series of fox-trot steps in unison. The Ladies team felt their confidence drain away when unexpectedly the M.C. announced an interlude of disco music. The team looked perplexed as the perspiring M.C. raced towards them and asked if he could have a quick word with the team leader.

'A twenty minute delay ladies,' Mrs Eckersby told them. 'It can't be helped.'

The two unmarried sisters in the team clung together for

support, their silver heads nodding. One began to fan the other's face, which had grown very pale.

'It's the tension,' she explained.' Our Sylvia can't take it.'

Ruby watched as the spectators began to pour onto the floor, pretending they could still do it.

A very heavy man shook himself around a much younger woman that Ruby guessed was his daughter. The desperation was tangible as dancers girated to prove they had what it took. Sweating men wiped their brows and plump, pink cheeked women in too-short skirts tried to keep up with the beat.

As she watched, someone seemed to slip and fall. Serves him right, she thought. Some damn' fool pretending to be a teenager. The music continued remorselessly,

I CANT GET NO SATIS FAK SHONE

while the dance band stood around the bar watching – the disco made more noise than they ever could.

Then Ruby realised that something was wrong. The person who had slipped seemed reluctant to get up. She watched his dark suit as it lay on the floor, dusted in moving lights from the crystal ball.

Couples stopped dancing. Someone screamed. The music ended abruptly as the M.C. grabbed the microphone. His voice over the tannoy pleaded for a doctor. The floor began to clear. No one came forward.

'A nurse or someone,' the tannoy urged while the manager strode out and stood over the prostrate suit and people helped the stunned, young partner away.

'Oh, that poor man, that poor man,' someone said and before she had time to think Ruby had stepped out there in full view of everyone in her beautiful dress and told the manager to get the first aid kit.

Ruby wouldn't let anyone move him until the ambulance arrived. First she knelt and listened for his heartbeat, then she tried the kiss of life after hearing a faint lub-dub in his chest. But the suit did not respond. She was terrified, but said nothing to the manager in case it was relayed to the partner. If the daughter went into a faint Ruby would never be able to cope. She whacked the man on the chest and felt her dress strain at the seams. She knelt across him and pounded, feeling the weak beat.

When the stretcher bearers arrived they insisted that someone accompany the man to hospital, and as the youthful partner was nowhere to be found, Ruby walked soberly behind the stretcher. It was her duty, even if it left her team a member short.

'We were that proud of you Ruby Harper,' Mrs Godison said back on the coach. 'Right proud.'

The team had done very well in Ruby's absence. They had received special commendation and an honorary award. In the formation dance Ruby's partner danced alone with a spotlight where the missing dancer ought to have been. Like they did the night Pavlova died, when, in a packed theatre, an empty spotlight followed the steps for Swan Lake.

'It was good all right,' another team member said. 'We told the M.C. you were our best dancer too. We got a standing ovation after we'd finished.'

Ruby's partner, in a flash of inspiration, had stood up from the group curtsey and pointed to the empty spotlight.

'The audience went mad clapping when she did that.'

Some of the team sniffed and reached for their handkerchiefs, recalling the emotion of the event. The two sisters leaned against each other and sobbed, overcome by the intensity of the moment.

'I'll never forget it,' Sylvia heaved, 'not till my dying day.'

'I'm proud of all of you,' Mrs Eckersby said. 'I've always said, one for all and all for one. We have strong links in our chain. We're professionals. You did a noble thing Mrs Harper.'

Someone asked what had happened to the man. Up till then they seemed to have forgotten about him.

'He was found dead on arrival at the hospital,' Ruby said flatly, and silence fell. It was a subdued coach party that travelled home. Ruby was glad of the silence, she needed to sleep.

While the others had been taken back to their hotel and had changed out of their frocks for a late dinner, Ruby had sat up in the waiting-room until the next of kin arrived – his wife, who screamed 'But he was on a business trip! What was he doing in a dance hall?' and would have flown at Ruby in her evening dress, but for an orderly getting between them.

Early the next morning Ruby was deposited on her doorstep. She turned and waved to the remaining team mates as she let herself in. Her blue frock was crushed and stained with perspiration. The hem was dark rimmed where it had swept the ground of the hospital forecourt.

She unzipped the frock. It would go to the cleaner's tomorrow, or was that today already?

She hung it in the wardrobe out of habit then she lay back on top of the bed and shut her eyes.

I'm sorry Jack. Tears of disappointment which she had held back until safely alone now trickled down her face. Her big night had been and gone. It would be months before they had another chance. She'd missed their first, big event and there could be no going back on that.

The absent dancer, that was her, a spotlight only for all the years she'd stopped dancing. Life was unfair. But there will be other times, she thought as she wiped her face. Don't fret Jack, you'll see me dancing again.

Exhaustion overtook her. Within minutes of lying back she was asleep.

In the wardrobe the crumpled blue dress danced easily with the three-piece suit. Free of that dragging, cumbersome boot at last, Jack's best suit moved into a tango, danced a rhumba, then a fox-trot, fastest of all. It swept the beautiful blue dress up and held its 1,000 fake pearls close to its breast pocket as together they spun in an endless dance that rose high over the silence of the sleeping house. High above the motionless figure on the bed.

Nancy and the Last Ever Monkey

I remember the late fifties in Liverpool when old people still had parrots. On warm days the heavy iron cages were hung outside and the street would fill with screeches. They were brought back by sailors, a relic of the city's seafaring past. That was when the docks still teemed with workers, when the quays rang to the bite of hooks and slap of sacking. That was before the containers arrived like coffins. Grim funeral barges ushering in the deathly stillness at the waterfront. The city held no wakes. It burned no fires. We did not know how to mourn our dead properly, so they could not leave. The docks never felt empty. It was a strange thing, but many of us noticed how you could stand all on your own listening to that odd silence yet still swear the docks were full of people, and all the sweat which wouldn't evaporate.

The workforce was moved from the old centre, towards the recent industrial estates. They left the elderly behind to sit clutching memories, alone with their exotic pets. There was no room for such relics in new council houses.

No one knew what to do when, one sunny morning in Kirkby, possibly the last ever monkey arrived. It came in a crate from Africa, marked all over with quarantine stickers.

The man from the customs swore as he signed the release paper.

'I'll be glad to see the back of that noisy so and so.' And he sucked his finger where the monkey had nipped it through the slats.

The delivery man left the crate on the door step.

'It's a bad-tempered bugger,' he told the Rourkes who had to sign for it.

They were too scared to lift the lid. They went next door to Nancy. Big, soft-hearted Nancy who took in strays.

'Look what he's gone and sent us now,' Mrs Rourke exclaimed,

Those Sailing Ships of His Boyhood Dreams

holding the crate at arm's length where it twisted and writhed.

'I can't let it out. I'm that scared.'

Nancy stood in the doorway with her coat on. She tied her headscarf firmly about her chin.

'Why don't you let it out in the garden, then it can run around. It might be like a rat if it's cornered,' she warned. 'I'll get it some bananas and things, while I'm at the market.'

When she returned with a shopping bag full of fruit the monkey was at least out of its box.

'We can't get it to come down,' Mrs Rourke wailed.

Nancy glanced up and saw the monkey swinging from a light flex.

'We put out a bowl of milk and a little piece of bread, but it just chewed it up into pellets and spat them at us.'

Mrs Rourke was terrified; her husband was due on the afternoon shift and she did not want to be left alone with it.

He sat lacing his boots up, slowly.

'I'll kill that lad of ours. What does he think he's playing at sending us a sodding monkey? If he thinks this is a joke, I'll kill him.' He tied the knots firmly and stood up.

Nancy broke a banana from the bunch. The monkey stopped twisting around the flex and watched. She held the fruit steady and began to pull back the yellow skin. The animal arched its back and stared. Nancy tried to fix it with a look as she had read in the RSPCA's dog-training manual. She held out the banana.

'Here boy.'

There was a blur as the creature jumped upon Mrs Rourke's shoulder. She screamed piercingly. The monkey did not respond to the sound, but sat stoically and reached out to take the banana from Nancy's shaking hand. Then it leapt back to the light flex where it was able to give the piece of fruit its undivided attention.

Mrs Rourke slithered into an arm chair in a state of shock. Her husband fanned her face. Her legs stuck out, unable to support her.

'Oh, God, it's like a little man.' she sobbed. 'I can't look at it. It's the hands I can't get used to. It's too human. It will be taking over.'

The monkey threw down the skin, then settled on the top of the china cupboard, where it could watch them from a height.

Nancy and the Last Ever Monkey

'Didn't it go out into the kitchen earlier and I was too nervous to go in after it. I had to shout for him to come and poke it with an umbrella.'

There was a loud knock on the door.

'We heard a terrible scream and wondered if everything was all right?'

Two women stood in the front patch of brown, untidy garden, shopping bags at the ready.

'You'd best come in,' Mr Rourke said and they thought he was about to make a full confession until they stepped into the parlour. One of the women yelped and blessed herself, while the other went down on her knees and would not look up.

'Oh God, its all that Satanism we've been reading about in the *News of the World*,' she wailed.' I've just seen the face of the devil!'

'Don't talk soft,' Mr Rourke told them. 'It's a monkey, that's what it is.'

While the discussion was going on around her, Nancy continued to offer bananas to the animal. She noticed that each time it came down to take one, it would remain slightly longer than before. When it ran the length of her arm and peered into her face, she stood her ground and tried to outstare it. When it finally caught hold of her and hugged her tightly, the hairs on the back of her neck stood up. Then it did the strangest thing. It climbed down inside the front of her coat and, settling like a baby, fell asleep. Everyone watched in silence. Nancy was rigid.

'What the hell do I do now?'

Her teeth were clenched.

'Oh, look. It's adopted you,' one of the neighbours said.

'Ah, isn't it sweet,' they agreed, now that it was still and silent.

'Oh, mum, isn't it wonderful?' Nancy's children whispered.

No one wanted to disturb it. They crept around on tiptoe. Nancy could not move.

'What the hell do I do?' she said again, and saw her children's upturned faces.

'Oh, no,' she said. 'We're not taking it in.'

Mr Rourke shook his head from side to side.

'I'll have to have it put down.'

'Oh, you wouldn't!' said his wife. Then, seeing the strange hard look he gave her, she changed her manner.

33

Those Sailing Ships of His Boyhood Dreams

'Well,' she coughed,' I expect it's for the best. He's quite right, it will have to be . . . ' her voice faltered as she looked to where it slept inside the front of Nancy's coat, 'you know. . . ' she finished lamely.

'Destroyed,' her husband boomed, and Nancy's children stood in front of their mother, a solid flank as if her life was threatened.

'Anything else I might consider, but a monkey, never.' Nancy said.

That night she listened for the sound of his boots crunching on the gravel path. In the front room the kids were watching television. The monkey had settled among them. It chattered and laughed and pointed to the screen.

She heard his key turn in the lock. She ought to head him off, but already he had his head around the door to say hello to the children. She stood in the kitchen waiting for the explosion, but heard nothing. He came out to her with a grin.

'Those little devils are up to something, I'm sure of it. You should have heard how they went silent when I looked around.'

'Oh yes?' Nancy asked.

She leant back against the cooker. A hungry man is an angry man, she told herself.

'I'll just put your tea out.'

She rushed past him, averting her eyes.

While he ate in the kitchen she slowly retraced his steps. She was too scared to go into the parlour, but stood outside hearing the children's voices, the television and the screech of inhuman laughter.

'Do you hear the racket in there?' he said, talking with his mouth full as she went back into the kitchen.

'Racket?' she said, watching him eat. She would have to tell him sometime.

'It must be a zoo programme,' he said.

'Well, actually,' Nancy began slowly, but she did not get past the first sentence. Her husband was staring beyond her. He saw a monkey enter the kitchen, climb up onto the cupboard and take down a cup from a hook and walk out, carrying this in front of it. His face drained of colour. His eyes swelled.

'Whatever is wrong?' she asked solicitously. 'You look dreadful. Are the spuds not cooked?'

That first Christmas, when Nancy's family opened their presents, the monkey got its share too. It pulled oranges from an old sock and scattered nuts everywhere, clapping its little paws together in delight. Nancy said that she could not bear to see its sad little face on Christmas morning otherwise.

The monkey was always cold, it constantly shivered and at first they had kept the electric fire on day and night, but the bill was horrendous so Nancy took to knitting it jumpers. That Christmas they all had matching Aran cardigans, and the monkey, who now went by the name of Thomas, looked extremely smart in his.

It went everywhere with the family because they could not let it stay in on its own. On Sundays it would accompany them to mass and every Wednesday it would go with Nancy on the weekly shopping trip. It would sit on the handles of Nancy's trolley and at the checkout it would help to load up. Then it might curl up, exhausted by all its efforts, and sleep the remainder of the way home. On the bus, Thomas was charged at half fare. At night he slept in a cardboard box at the foot of the twins' bed.

They were busy days. The overtime was there for the taking. Families were still moving out to the new towns. The monkey chattered and screeched. To Nancy life was bright. She understood that hard work brought rewards; the first battered car they bought took them out to West Kirkby, and out to the sand dunes at Ainsdale. They drove in those prosperous days into a better life than the one they had left behind in the smoky, overcrowded inner city. This was the new world, they were the new people, with healthy children and a garden for them to play in. A monkey ran up and down the stairs of a council house and there was such a feeling of optimism.

But things did not stay the same. One day, the monkey, playing happily in the garden, was frightened by something. Nancy never knew what it was, a neighbour's dog, a bird, possibly a shadow; but whatever it was caused the animal to jump up and run along the uppermost branches of the tree. It screeched and shrieked while she called to it. The thin top branches bent under the monkey's fragile weight. It clung to them desperately.

No amount of coaxing would get him down this time. Always a quick animal, she was surprised that he had not been lost before. It used to dash off, run up walls, but had always been glad to take the arm held out to it, to jump back into the careful hands. This time it was obstinate. It shook its tiny head and chattered.

The children called to it, but Nancy knew that they had seen the last of the monkey as it jumped onto the guttering and climbed up onto the roof. It kept moving. Stepping ever further away from them, it leapt to the adjoining roof and gathering speed, cleared one garden after the other. They saw its tail for a last second, flying high and proud, and then it disappeared.

All night the children were inconsolable and he even went to the bottom of the garden with a torch. He tramped over plants in his wellingtons calling softly, 'Thomas, Thomas . . . ' The following morning when the children came down she shook her head at their unspoken question. They cried over their uneaten bowls of cornflakes and were a slow, miserable straggle as they left for school. For almost a fortnight, every time they heard a noise in the garden, they ran out expecting to find Thomas and every evening as her husband hung up his coat he would look hopefully at Nancy, who shook her head each time. For those first weeks the children dragged their feet and hung about indoors, bored with themselves and each other, then slowly they forgot Thomas the way that children can.

'They've got over it, thank God!' he said when he saw them playing happily again. But Nancy knew they would never recapture that time. After Thomas left the days somehow felt different. Not just because there was no excited screech, no mad scampering on the landing. There was a stillness that she could not adjust to and the mood outside altered. When she shopped each Wednesday it was in a bored way. She resented the tedium of the same shops, the same faces. Now whenever she stood in her garden, all she saw were things which needed fixing. Rusted spouting, the great damp patch on the back wall, frames which warped and made windows impossible to open. She thought she could see the steady subsidence of the house, and imagined it sinking further each day. For the first time she felt that everything had been thrown together in a hurry, built on the cheap. And she knew that just like the monkey, nothing was intended to last.

Maeve the Broken-hearted

'He broke her heart. What a dirty, low down trick that was.' Her mouth set in a look of disgust. Then she remembered that he had been my father. Her eyes flickered upwards and she started to apologise. 'Well life is messy. Look at me own.'

Her husband left her when the kids grew up. He'd been planning it for years, ever since his return from the war with nerves torn to match the frayed edges of ribbon on medals he never received.

'I've been through so much.' Her voice trembled but she didn't cry. 'But him.' She shook her head. 'Him!' She saved her energy for my father, the Him of her youth.

'Maeve was beautiful then. Well, she was a fine woman. But she was almost too fine. Too reserved. She hung back. She'd never meet anyone. Well, where would she? There was nowhere to go, not then, not for single women. Only tarts went into the other kind of places. Like the rest of us she worked during the day. We'd organise something, get a group up from work, but she was always too shy. I reckon she spent more nights at home than me mam did, and she'd had a stroke. Maeve should have been out enjoying her youth. But there was only her and your mother left at home. We were all married and then your mam went to work the summer stretch in Llandudno; that was the time she stayed with Aunt Nora,' she added by way of explanation. But I knew the story, knew it well. Could have recited how Mam came back in winter to meet the boy she'd known in Belfast before they moved.

It was like a fairy story how my father turned up all those years later, looking for the girl he'd been at school with. So they got together at last as if fate was being moved by his will. In the normal course of events he would have been a distant memory, but he was not happy with that version so he turned the plan around, appearing where the family lived. And he kept appearing.

Those Sailing Ships of His Boyhood Dreams

He re-introduced himself to her mother and by the time Mam returned from Llandudno, he and Gran were bosom friends.

He would push the old one out into the yard on sunny days and he was always ready to knock loose slates back into place, to nail and hammer and climb up onto the roof and see what needed fixing. It all sounded straightforward to me, but I could tell by the way my Aunt Beatty couldn't sit still that there had been something else. Was that it? The phrase, He broke her heart? Whose heart?

'Do you want more tea?' Beatty asked me for the umpteenth time. The oldest sister who had outlived all of them. Last Christmas she sent me a card, and wrote on it 'I'm the only one left'. Whenever I phone her she cries. My mother always used to get the whisky out when she came round, now when I go to her, she always has a bottle waiting. A tradition. We drink and laugh, remembering. Sometimes she'll sing. Viva España, The Crystal Chandeliers, Does Anybody Here Know Kelly. She fair belts it out at her age. We're limbering up with tea and Swiss roll.

'It'll put a lining on your stomach.'

She goes into the kitchen and bangs the kettle around. I hear her muttering, 'Broke her heart, broke her bloody heart.'

'Me Gran's?' I ask her as she returns carrying a metal tray with pictures of overfed cats round the border.

'Are you wise?' she stops and puts the tray on the coffee table. 'Our Maeve. He broke her heart. Sly he was. That's what he did with all that intelligence they always reckoned he had. Aye, well, I suppose your father was brainy, but what's the point of brains if you haven't the wit to see what's going on?'

This was a new twist. I remember that he had little time for any of Mam's family after Gran died.

'There's none of them worth bothering with, except for Gran, God rest her.' And every evening he closed the front door behind him and was happy if no one came through it. 'Only for your gran,' he'd say. 'You're like her to look at,' and his eyes would become soft.

But Beatty always said that I was a dead ringer for Maeve when she was young. He'd have none of that.

'There's not a shave of that woman in her.'

I was in my teens before I realised how acute was their dislike

Maeve the Broken-hearted

of one another. I was told that Maeve had left the district when my mother was expecting me and had not returned until all the babies were born.

I was six or seven when this glamorous new aunt swept into our lives, smelling of rose-water and powder. She was a frequent visitor during work hours when my father was out, but at five-thirty she would start to gather her things together and go, disappearing just as the works bus dropped my father at the corner. We would see him swinging his cutting-up tin as he came down the street Aunt Maeve had just fled along.

Indoors he would put the empty tin on the sideboard where it would sit until my mother said, 'I've to do your father's cutting-up,' and she would pull herself out into the kitchen.

It seemed to me that she reserved that chore for the ends of films she was watching, because she kept missing the closing scenes, those moments of revelation where the mystery was at last uncovered. The following morning one of us always had to go through what happened while she listened with an air of martyrdom and muttered about 'woman's lot' as she filled the kettle. Sometimes she might leave the tin and wait until she was dropping from exhaustion and he was on his way to bed. Then she'd shout after him on the stairs.

'I'd go up to bed myself, but I've the cutting-up to do.'

None of us could be trusted to do it. We were too young to handle knives, then as we grew, too stupid. It was her penance.

Once, early in the morning, I crept down before the whistle sounded. The tin was on the table in the grey dawn, mysterious as Pandora's box. I tiptoed on soft feet. The lid was yellow enamel, chipped at the corners, and it lifted easily as I carefully prised it up, hoping no one would hear.

Inside, wrapped in loaf paper, were the magical things my mother laboured to create. Corned beef on white sliced bread, a small Kit-Kat and an apple for him to practise his new false teeth on.

I looked under the sandwiches hoping to find at least a message, maybe different kinds of food, protein pills like spacemen took. There was nothing. I put the lid back on the ordinariness of our lives. Heartbroken wasn't the word for me that day.

But not as heartbroken as Maeve had been according to Aunt

Beatty. And this was news to me.

'How do you mean, he broke her heart? My father? But they couldn't stick each other.'

'It was the time your mother was away. He arrived, a stranger, new to the place and he just stood there. I can see him now. He asked if Ann Pearce lived there and did anyone remember him at all, only he'd heard the family'd moved.

'He'd been up and asked the parish priest because he knew my dad died the year before. He didn't ask for him, you see, because he already knew. He was smart, I'll give him that.

'But that was the time Annie was away. Only Maeve was at home then, looking after me mother. He used to call up. Oh, he was a proper gentleman, do you know what I mean? He was very polished your father. Had lovely manners outside the house. Inside it ...' she shrugged. 'He had a temper didn't he? He was strict. He brought you up right.'

'He was more than strict,' I told her, remembering the grey, humourless man who came home from work one night covered in soot. There was a terrible smog that year and all the buses went off because the Corporation didn't want to be responsible for accidents. They let the men out early so they could find their way home.

My father was too proud to ask anyone for a lift. He walked all the way from the industrial estate. It was late and I remember how Mother paced the floor and slapped us all in turn.

'Don't be bloody well annoying me!' she yelled all evening and her hand came down across any waiting face.

When he walked in she said he looked like a miner. He'd held a scarf over his mouth and he'd had to keep stopping to wipe his glasses.

It got into his lungs. Mam said he was never the same man again. First his chest, then later his heart. He would take a long time recovering that winter. But once he'd been fit and he used to laugh.

'He swept her off her feet.'

'My mother?' I grinned, trying to imagine anyone shaking her from her lethargy, upsetting the tired woman I knew.

'Good God no, although I'm sure he did that as well. No, I'm talking about our Maeve.'

Aunt Beatty started brushing up crumbs from the carpet. Her elbows stuck out and her body vibrated as she raked fluff into the dust pan.

'What did my father ever have to do with Aunt Maeve?' I asked. 'He despised her.'

'That's what I'm after telling you. He just turned up out of nowhere. An unknown quantity. And he seemed to be interested in her. He took her out – dancing, the pictures. You should have seen her then. She did blossom, thinking she might have a life, that she could see a future, an escape. And he was great with our mam, I'll give him that. He made her happy. He was different, not like the local types, who'd never been good enough for our Maeve. But this stranger was. And we were all delighted for her.

'Then your mam returned from Nora's and his attention just switched. We could see that he'd only used Maeve to get into our mam's good books, because by now she could see no wrong in him. He was charming when he wanted something. The miserable sod! You'll have to excuse me, I keep forgetting he was your dad.'

She knelt up on the carpet. Her face was level with mine as I sat in the armchair.

'Maeve was proud. It must have felt as if she'd been thrown over for the younger sister. It must have hurt her terribly. She went away. Left them to it. But her feelings turned to hate. I'd see her watching him sometimes and her eyes would be narrowed like a cat's into two grey slits.

'None of us could be bothered with him after that. Your mother was always tough, but Maeve wasn't. It's dangerous to play with people's feelings. You never know how they'll react. Anybody else might have got over it, but she couldn't. It broke her. I suppose he couldn't have foreseen that, but then he didn't consider anyone's feelings. He seemed to think he could do just as he liked. But after, when Annie understood, she turned cold towards him. She seemed to lose respect for him. Like I said, she was tough your mother, she never let her feelings show, even before that, she'd never let him see if she cared for him, and after, well, I suppose she didn't really. The only one who felt for him was your poor aunt, and so she nursed her grudge until it seemed to choke her.

Those Sailing Ships of His Boyhood Dreams

'There was a man later, wanted to marry her, but she hurt him. She laughed at his proposal, which came in a letter, because he couldn't spell. Your father was an educated man.' She nodded at me.

'But your mother didn't get a better deal. She was never happy. You could tell, just by watching them together. They hardly spoke to each other. Well, he'd try, God help him. He was besotted with your mother, you know, the poor sod. But he'd ruined it for everyone. She couldn't be bothered with him really. Lived with him on sufferance.'

'They were always arguing behind closed doors,' I told her. Aunt Beatty smiled.

'Yes, we all knew. It was the Third World War. That's what your mother called it. You know,' she said, 'your Aunt Maeve would always go up there to defend Annie. She was always the one who helped her to pack her bags. She wanted Annie away from him, so he could be on his own and know what that felt like. But he knew what it felt like. He was on his own in that marriage. Maeve used to go up when he was at work and help your mother compose the definitive goodbye note. Only your mother could never carry it through.'

How I remembered that. The coats and hats pulled on too quickly. Instructions shouted at us to leave everything and get out of the house. The half-walk, half-run to the bus stop, mother watching for any of the neighbours who might ask where we were going, and the paper carrier bags with our clothes in, spilling out onto the street.

And it was always Maeve who gave us a welcome, who put us up in her backroom and sat through the night over pots of tea with her weeping sister.

I used to be terrified those nights. I would lie awake shivering. Once I found myself out on the landing, with no idea how I'd got there. I remember creeping downstairs where a crack of yellow light showed under the door. I tried to look in through the key hole, but could see nothing, so I pushed the door open a fraction and waited. They didn't see me. My mother was sobbing. She sat sprawled over the table with her head in her hands. My aunt was standing up, stroking her sister's dark hair which straggled over the white skin of her arms. Then I remembered the look on

Maeve's face. I couldn't understand it then. It disturbed me.

Maeve was staring into the distance. She looked content, calm. Suddenly she smiled. Her whole face was transfigured. It was a look of triumph. My mother glanced up from the table and Maeve's expression altered, the smile vanished.

She was the one we always went to, rather than the others.

'Maeve knows, she understands,' my mother used to say. We were scared and silent.

'The miserable sod. He broke her heart. Let me pour the tea.'

Beatty straightened up. She rubbed her knees and took my saucer from the arm rest where I'd balanced it.

'I've got some eclairs, they were our poor Maeve's favourites. Or would you like some more Swiss roll?'

'I'm not fussed.'

She went back into the kitchen looking for a knife. When she returned she brought me a Kit-Kat.

'I didn't know that about my father,' I said as I unwrapped it. 'I'd no idea about Maeve.'

Being careful not to drop crumbs on the carpet I snapped the fingers in two. To my surprise they didn't scatter bits of chocolate all over the plate, but broke cleanly, as if they were illustrating a point.

Three Views From a House

The sun never shone on that half of the road, and the house was just unfortunate to be on the wrong side. She herself was a hard woman who never smiled and said that life was purgatory. She moved through the damp grey rooms never sitting in any. She could not enjoy the day which was left to her once all her work was done. It was the worst part of the day. Unfit for anything, but good enough for the likes of . . . But she always had a broom or a mop in her hand, announcing to the outside world that she still worked hard. Just because she was widowed, there was no reason to let all go to hell. Now her life's reason was to keep everything neat. She felt satisfaction when she ached because the floors were scrubbed. If she sat still she could hear her own thoughts. She polished her emotions until they shone, worn away after years like the wooden figure in the church the faithful touched until he had no face. No eyes to stare with, just as hers could not see that day when he took her hand to show the ring for posterity. He lifted her hand up for the photographer and it was no longer hers.

Now she only touched things to clean them, seeing everything as the cause of dust. No other contact was allowed. And she infected everything with her anger, and her unhappiness. Her heart was tight inside her, shrinking.

She watched the moon waning in the yard, a thin crescent disappearing into soft blue night. And she had wanted to sink back into the blue silk of the photographer's studio. But instead she had just let her hand be lifted, and she made a smile, cruel as a sharp moon for the camera. During the day the photograph mocked her from the sideboard.

She woke from what felt like a deep sleep and wondered what time it was. She felt warm, although she did not know whether she was indoors or out until she saw the high ceiling. Daylight and traffic and voices all poured in the open curtains. Why wasn't she rushing? Where should she be? She lay feeling dazed, trying to work out her next move.

Over her head she watched discoloured damp spots grouping into shapes. Faces stared down, some friendly, some curious, but none of them threatening. Unlike those chalk men of her childhood. They were the faces which appeared each time her teacher wiped the blackboard. Horrible, twisted beings stared back at her. They would stare right at her desk and she knew they were threatening to tell, to shout out Liar! Thief! Cheat! Those monstrous childhood accusations that would stick. Names that once given could not be erased like the chalk letters on the board. She was scared they would steal her character, by a phrase, by telling, or just by a look. A doubt, a hint was worse than anything. It would grow in the darkness of her classmates' imagination. Then she would never be the same.

She once had a childhood. What was the name of the woman who taught her? She could see her face but for the life of her couldn't remember what she was called. Couldn't think of the name of the school either. Terrible to forget a place where she had spent so many miserable years. She remembered the misery, not the name. In the city. She used to walk to it, along grey cobbled streets. And the rooms were draughty. Cold all year not only winter.

Today was ... she did not know. It seemed as if it had all happened before. There was a familiarity about the strange place she woke in. Before she lifted her head she already knew the position of the door. She knew that the windows were on the furthest wall. It was curious. She ought to be scared.

She sat up slowly. She had been kidnapped, but as soon as the thought came, she laughed at the absurdity of it. Well then, she had been drugged. Again, another surge of mirth. She might have been dazed, but she was letting her imagination run off with her. For what purpose? She knew what she was, an elderly female of average height, turning to fat with terrible feet which must have suffered a lifetime of badly fitting shoes. Her hands were broad and rough. Worker's hands. She knew she couldn't be a classical pianist. She wore a gold band and an engagement ring. Well that was a clue. She would just sit in and wait for the

Three Views From a House

husband to return and tell her who she was.

She sat up on the bed. It was a high old-fashioned thing that they must have bought out of necessity rather than for its looks. Dark black wood.

She was surprised at how far away the floor seemed. It was bare except for the cold green and olive patched lino. Had she woken into another time? These things came from her childhood. But the coverlet on the bed was bright pink. She had been lying on top of it, fully dressed. The counterpane was flounced and nylon. It was slipping off the top of the bed, hopeless nylon is. But modern. She wondered if that was her doing.

As she swung her legs down she noticed the massive wardrobe which faced her. Black wood with carvings and a winged fancy thing over the mirror. She recognised herself in that. She was not alarmed by her appearance. She looked as she imagined she would. Of course her hair was grey.

When she looked around, she knew that she had always detested the big lumps of wooden furniture. They were not to her taste at all. She would have preferred something lighter, more modern, something out of pale blond wood. She must have had that bed and wardrobe for years. This was her home then, not a hospital ward or a friend's house. It was hers.

Traffic went past one window, but the other looked out onto a quieter side street. Outside, she saw a pavement and a single tree. There was no garden. It would be her luck to be reincarnated into a terraced house. She would never wake up in a stately home and grounds. Maybe not this time around. Maybe she was a time traveller. Wise up . . . Girl . . . she had no name to give herself. She could still stop being fanciful, if she had left her name somewhere, she had not left her common sense.

Before that last sleep she must have understood the world she lived in. All she needed was a name, with it she would make sense of her surroundings. Everything would fit into place. Her husband would return and tell her. It was day, so he was at work. That made sense. He would come home in the evening. She would find the kitchen, cook a meal. That made sense. She would explore the house. He'd talk and she would be able to put the pieces together. Find out who she was. She would reassemble her past.

Those Sailing Ships of His Boyhood Dreams

And what might he be like? She had been with him a long time, the ring was immovable on her swollen finger. A lifetime. They probably had grown-up children. Maybe they had a child still at home.

She opened the door. The house was silent. Ahead of her stretched a dark landing and a flight of stairs. Two doors led off to the left. Stepping out silently, she touched a switch and was horrified to see a bare bulb. She would get that sorted out. The landing smelt musty. Somewhere there was damp. Those patches on the ceiling were signs of greater disrepair. She would get him to see to it.

The wallpaper along the landing was dark green, and in a style she had not seen since childhood when everyone had picture rails and a wall frieze of white to surround the ceiling. Yet the bedroom she left had been papered with a textured surface and whitened. It was brighter in there because of the white walls and the pink counterpane. She felt that must have been her doing. But this landing was dreadful, as if they had not bothered. The closed doors were worrying. She knocked on one.

The house was perfectly quiet, except for the sounds of traffic. Even the air seemed to hang, solid, waiting for someone to disturb it. It felt as if no one had been there for a long time. She pushed the door on the landing open. She knew the window would face her.

In the room was a bare bed, no more than a mattress on legs really. A few battered suitcases and a wardrobe that had been painted white. Some dusty, soft toys sat on a high shelf, staring down at her. Nothing jogged her memory. Inside the wardrobe was a curious mixture of young and old things. A shiny, narrow black mac hung right at the back. Not hers, it wouldn't have gone near her. There were long dresses, with floral prints and some kind of Indian embroidery. An orange kaftan. That's what you call them, she thought. But in the front there were rows of normal looking skirts, with huge waistbands. They were hers. Someone had left home. This must have been the room of ... who ... a daughter certainly, but where was she now?

The second room, when she plucked up courage to enter it, was worse. A complete mess, with an ironing board and a pile of clothes dumped on the floor, a sewing machine by the window on a small table, and some unfinished curtains strewn beside it. She hated sewing, because of the mess it made. There were threads of cotton all over the floor, slivers of material from doing hems. Well she wasn't going to finish them.

The bed was turned upright against the wall. Not even a semblance of a wardrobe but a tall cupboard. She turned drawers out. Nothing. Scraps of paper, sweet wrappers, and dust. In some drawers sheets, and carefully folded blankets. Again, this felt like a spare room. Once used, now vacated. There were some books on otherwise empty shelves. Poetry and science fiction. A tennis racquet against the wall, a pair of football boots and a telescope. A son. Who was he? Where was he?

She walked downstairs, unable to find the light switch for the lower landing, and although it was day outside, no window lit up the lower stairwell which was gloomy and frightening. A row of three black circular switches were lined on top of each other by a door. To her right there was a dark curtain and behind it, coats hanging. Tucked in there, a telephone and beside it on a ledge, an address book.

She could read this, maybe phone someone in the book, ask them if they knew her. But she couldn't phone up without a name. Suppose someone asked. Who should she say she was? What could she say? And then people might get the wrong idea, decide she was crazy, not merely forgetful, not merely confused. If she could just remember a few things, she had no doubt that the rest of her life would fit back together.

She glanced up to the higher ceiling of the top landing, up through the stairwell and for a moment had a recollection of people disappearing up into darkness.

In a dark gymnasium, ropes appear from nowhere. The gym mistress is shouting herself hoarse. A girl stands there staring up to where her friends are disappearing, vanishing into the oriental trick, and she knows that she will never manage it.

Curl your foot round, Use your arms, the instructor shouts and she hangs limply from the rope with one toe touching the gym's wooden floor, unable to go any higher. All around her girls vanish, in straight lines. They rise and climb to the dark tops of ropes. But she is left. Alone, her foot touches the ground.

Those Sailing Ships of His Boyhood Dreams

The last door to be opened was white. Like the others it was smooth finished and it opened into a living room with a tiny kitchen space in the back. Along the corridor was the front door, but she would not brave that now. She heard something lift. Did someone have a key? Her heart skipped in her chest and she tried to remain calm. But whoever it was had gone away. Out of the window she saw a postman. She ran to the doormat, You have been chosen to take part in our free draw. The occupier. But she knew the name of her street. Knew the number she lived in. That was something. If she could find a key she might go out, have a look around. Without a key, she might never get back in. And if she got lost ... she would have to write the address down, and make a note of the telephone number, so at least she had some particulars.

In the kitchen there was a fridge. An open carton of milk, half-empty, still usable, sat in the bottom. Some cheese spreads and boxes. She realised that she was simply starving and began to ransack the cupboards for something to eat. Lots of tins, packets of instant this and that. In the freezer, beefburgers, fish fingers, instant meals, reheat, for people in a hurry. Whoever she was she didn't like cooking. The quality of the food depressed her. Instant meals for one. She lived alone. It began to hit her, slowly and horribly. This was her house. Her husband, whoever he was, had died. She was a widow. The widow what? If only she could give herself a name.

She didn't like it. Was this her second life, like a cat has nine? Had she used one already and been thrown this to finish off? This felt like an ending, not a beginning.

She fried burgers, opened a tin of beans, fried an egg, sliced the remains of a loaf she found in the bread bin, still fresh. She made tea, after hunting for the pot. It was reassuring and familiar. This was what she usually did she told herself. But it was so dull, so regular, there was nothing exotic. Was this her reward after a lifetime that she could not even remember?

In the living room she put up the drop-leaf table, having spent some time working it out, and sat to eat her solitary meal. Day. An electric clock said 12:30. Noon. She hadn't gone to pieces all together. She still had some order. It was noon and she was having lunch.

What would she do for the rest of the afternoon? What used she to do before ... There were cupboards and mysterious looking boxes. She pulled out a jewel box, lots of cut glass and cheap paste, bright pretty things which she diverted herself with for an hour, watching the effect in the mirror. Only clip-on ear-rings. Nothing pierced. That was good. The idea of holes in her ears made her sick. These were her ear-rings, that was her old feeling. She was excited, recognising something about herself.

In a cupboard were receipts for bills. Of course, they would be addressed ... she started to look through them ... a name. Initials. B. D. Davey. She stared, expecting this to trigger a response. But nothing happened. B. D. What could they mean? Davey. Mrs Davey. A widow, she was certain. The name left her strangely unaffected. Nothing. No sudden rush. A stranger's name. At least she paid her bills promptly. She dreaded the idea of being in debt. She ought to be grateful. She might have discovered B. D. Davey owed hundreds. Worse, she might have been a bank robber. Thank God the ends left to her were neat.

On the sideboard a photo, a young woman in old-fashioned clothes and a man in a pin-striped suit. Just the two of them. They stood in front of a curtain. There was the studio stamp. The woman wore a day dress, yet she carried a bouquet of flowers. Her smile seemed uneasy. The man held her left hand holding the ring out to view. Just married. This was a wedding photograph, but there were no friends, no family. He didn't smile. And she knew it was her and he was her husband. Thick dark hair. And she didn't like the look of him at all.

She tries to stand up straight, but her new shoes are killing her. The photographer wants her to smile, he tells her to relax, but fails to tell her how. She wonders what he must make of them, the odd pair. She is much younger than the dark, unsmiling man who calls her his wife. It all feels so new, and uncomfortable.

These will be the official wedding photographs that they will send back to her husband's family. To the relatives she has not met. He says there is plenty of time for that. Now he touches her hand and holds it out so the ring glints. She lets her hand be manipulated. He does not speak, just takes her hand as he might an empty glove. Suddenly, hot tears prick her eyes and she hears him saying, 'Not again, you ruined all the photos of the ceremony. Can't you stop crying for once?' The man with the camera, looks over the top at her. He wants to know whether he should go on. She bares her teeth and grins. He holds her hand out. She tries to stare at the camera, but it has smudged and is dissolving. Please, she prays, take the picture now. Have done with it.

Behind her there are blue silk curtains, a beautiful blue. She thinks it is a shame that in the print they will only be grey.

In the kitchen she found a complete canteen of silver cutlery, unused, still in its velvet presentation box. What sort of a life had she, when even a canteen of cutlery was too good for her? She wished she'd found it earlier. She would have used the knives and forks for her burgers and beans. She turned the box upside down, shook it until everything tumbled out into the kitchen drawer, mixing up with plastic spoons and knives with burnt handles, in a jumble, nothing matching, and the dull silver lost with everyday utensils.

In the evening, she sat in the dark, listening for another sound of life. The street was quiet. No one came to her door. The names in the address book meant nothing to her, but inside the cover of Mrs Beaton's Practical Cookery written in pencil, Brenda Long. Brenda Long loves ? Marcia. Marcia Doctors is crossed out in scribble.

Marcia giggles and her blonde curls shake. Mrs MaGregor the Cookery teacher does not miss a trick and is down on them. She asks them what is so amusing but they can't speak for fright. Marcia splutters it out. The handle of the knife came clean away in her hand, Miss. The blade stuck in the dough. Somewhere it's still inside. Even Mrs MaGregor laughs. And she isn't afraid, but looks up at her teacher, who seems human now, her face creased with amusement. She stares at the floured board where the dough should be divided into two equal portions. Marcia asks should they bake it with the blade inside, Miss, and take it round to a prisoner? and the class laughs. Mrs MaGregor wraps it in newspaper and takes it out to the bin. They can sit out the rest of the lesson, and make up their note books. From the ovens the smell of baking bread is wonderful.

Marcia was the first girl up the Indian rope trick, who came back down laughing and said that it was safe. Marcia Doctors. Great times they had. Look under D. Under D. Doctor. Doctors, see Bailey. Mrs Bailey, how amusing! Call her, speak to her. Someone remembered. Remember me? Tell her, A Funny Thing happened. Have a laugh about it. Laugh together, old white curls shaking. Full of life, Mad Marce. Used to have them all in hysterics, used to mimic their headmistress. B. D. Davey that was once Brenda Long remembered. They wore dark green uniforms. Grey woollen stockings that itched. Marcia, cheer me, save me.

On the other end of the phone a young voice speaks. B. D. Davey who was Brenda Long says, 'I'm a friend of your mother's,' and speaks her new name as if it was always hers. 'We were at school together, just calling her up.'

'How kind. Mother's comfortable.'

No this isn't what it should be like. Madcap Marcia comfortable. Madcap Marce not able to come to the phone.

'What did you say your name was? It's good to know people haven't forgotten her.'

'How is she?'

'No significant change. Since the last stroke. Don't know whether she hears us or not. No response, not since the last one. Breathing regular. Nurse here all day, and one of us always here. Can't leave her alone, see?'

Brenda Long sits in the dark because Brenda Long is scared to sleep. And she is waiting for morning, as memory returns. She does not welcome memory, because it brings her back to face the empty day, and the one which will follow it.

Both my parents have been dead for so long that the wallpaper peels in their bedroom.

It was always too large a room, designed to terrify children. Now it is empty. White windows, grey light. Clouds pass outside. Waiting for the day when the walls are punched out and they can float through unhindered.

In the place where the wardrobe stood for years, the wall is discoloured and clutches at the empty shape. A dark, ungainly thing, she always said the house must have been built round it. Later, workmen smashed it in order to bring it out. The wallpaper, remembering the hammer, has bruised around the edges, and crouches, wishing it could hide again behind the great back.

Those Sailing Ships of His Boyhood Dreams

There are four marks on the floor, dug into the lino. These represent the weight-bearing legs of the bed. That too was solid. Immovable with secrets that were lodged in metal boxes and hidden underneath. Four pockmarks are all that's left of miserable nights, the habitual digging of years. The floor is scarred, resisting as she did, the woman who once told me about duty, and the correct way for a man and woman to be together, bound by have-to's, and must's, and God-given laws.

Once after gin and Guinness at Christmas, the woman said she thought there was 'something wrong with him' and said 'he couldn't' and said 'you know'. She talked about 'decent women' and long recurring nightmares of being suffocated, and said 'isn't that peculiar now?' and said 'no decent woman could'. She didn't look at me then, returning to her private, silent world where all the decent women shuddered to perform their duty.

Four scars are all that remain of her cold stigmata. They mark the place of suffering. This was her Golgotha and I kneel and touch them like a pilgrim coming onto holy ground.

The young woman got into the house by the kitchen window. It was never secure even when it was lived in. Workmen had boarded up the windows of the bottom floor, but she was able to prise a loose one up, and enter through this small window that once looked out onto the back yard. She carried a torch, because the bottom half of the house would be in darkness, even though it was daylight. She went from room to room, looking. In the living room the cold grate still had the last fire's ashes. The tiles around it had been broken. She bent and pulled up three from the floor that were loose. One was almost complete. It was a deep blue glaze with the figure of a soaring bird. She looked around, satisfied her curiosity.

Climbing out, a workman spotted her in the entry. He shouted that the whole row behind was dangerous. 'I wouldn't come down here for a short cut girl,' he yelled, and pointed with his thumb to the row of houses. 'That street's coming down,' he said.

'What's going to happen here?'

'Demolition,' he shouted over the traffic. 'That's the orders.'

'Is anything going to be built here?'

'I wouldn't know,' he shrugged. The young woman crossed to where he stood and looked back.

'Should have been pulled down years ago,' he told her. 'But there was someone still there. Couldn't get them out. An old person.'

The young woman walked off, hugging her tiles under her jacket. She wondered what it was like to be the last person living in a street of empty houses. All the doors boarded up, blind windows, and you alone with memories instead of neighbours.

*The O'Touney Sisters and the
Day of Reckoning*

My mother wouldn't go out of the house without Saint Anthony of Padua. Not since the time he had saved her from drowning in a bog.

'It's not every day a saint reaches out and plucks you from the jaws of hell,' she always said.

She kept him in her handbag. A travelling Saint Anthony, no bigger than a lipstick, he fitted into his own case.

The first time she left Ireland, newly married to my father, he was the saint who accompanied her on the journey to the godless land.

'He didn't stop me being seasick,' she told us. 'He hasn't the cure at all. Still, I wouldn't be without him.' Her arthritic fingers would stroke the slim metal case inside which the quiet silver statue nestled. He was the perfect travelling companion and the two of them went everywhere together.

My mother believed until her death that she owed her life to him. She was a devout Catholic whose faith was never shaken, unlike her sister who was an atheist. That, in any case, is what my mother called my aunt, although it's hard to see how she could be described as such. Brid never stopped believing in God, it was just that she hated him.

Each summer throughout my childhood we returned to Roscommon and my mother would no sooner have set foot in the old kitchen, but the rows between her and Brid would start.

She was always telling my aunt to mend her ways, to save her soul before it was too late. But Brid was adamant.

'You and your Saint Anthony,' she'd say. 'He might have pulled you clear, but he'd only strength enough for one of us,' and she used to gaze out of the back window towards the distant hills, where sky and earth touched briefly.

Those Sailing Ships of His Boyhood Dreams

'Go on, you heathen. You're walking around alive today,' my mother would scold her. But Brid just said it was a funny sort of life at that.

'What I have ever done?' she'd ask. 'I've never been anywhere. I don't get to see foreign places.'

Once the priest was arranging a visit to Fatima, but knowing my aunt's views on religion he did not offer her the chance.

'You can stay with us whenever you like,' my mother always remonstrated. And Brid would ask who was going to keep house for Titus when she was away. 'It's all right for you,' she always said, 'you and your Saint Anthony.'

Brid was my spinster aunt. She kept house for her brother. There had been, before I was born, a time when uncle Titus was walking out with the tailor's daughter. It came to nothing. My mother said Brid had a hand in the business. She could not have tolerated another woman in the kitchen.

I grew up hearing different stories about the Anthony of Padua rescue. Brid always referred to it as 'The Day Liddy Marnoch Gave Hospitality'. This was my great aunt. An old photograph and a reputation for meanness were all I knew of her.

'God, but she'd not give you a drop of tea if you'd had your throat cut.'

On her stinginess they were all agreed. It was said that she'd serve up plain boiled potatoes and hide the salt so that no one would have the taste for more than a couple.

'It was a penance going to visit her,' Titus used to say.

Their mother, my grandmother, had quarrelled with Liddy and used to yell that she would not have any of them going to see 'that woman'. She would not use her name.

'Why your uncle Jack married her is a mystery,' she would say. 'She's no aunt to any of you, all she ever wants you for is cheap labour.'

Usually they only went to the house if they knew their uncle might be home, otherwise Liddy would have them working round the house for her. But then she had no one to help around the place. In the one yellowed photograph that survives of her she is a thin unsmiling woman, as tight as a bit of flax. Her womb inherited her meanness so that her household would always have to rely on hired labour.

The O'Touney Sisters and the Day of Reckoning

And Liddy was houseproud – always busy with a routine of polishing and dusting, of sweeping and washing. She never stood still for a moment, as with elbow grease, she rubbed out the emptiness of her days. They all agreed that even her kitchen was like a palace and I would imagine it to be like one of the great, ruined castles we were brought out to see during the holidays. It must have felt a cold, hard place like the ancient seats of the kings of Ireland that were long empty, their subjects dispossessed, their winding cries left to sound against ruined walls and echo down the hollow years. And freezing. Liddy never lit the hearth until it was time for Jack to come home. She said it was a waste of good turf just for herself, but she'd watch visitors shivering and never light a stick for their comfort. The only time the kettle was put on was at the sound of his boots.

It wasn't reticence had her this way. My father once told me that her cake, whenever you were lucky enough to get a bit, was the best in the county. And her bread they described in unison as being more like scone, but she kept it under lock and key in the press and would only bring in a few slices at a time. They said it was a marvel to see how she could spread a piece and still keep a knife full of butter. How she managed to cut bread so thin was an art she had developed over years.

'If you held it up to the window you could see your hand through it,' Titus said.

On the day of the disputed miracle, my mother and aunt, both young girls then, had set out to walk to Liddy's. Knowing they'd get nothing until Jack arrived home they took with them a bottle of cold tea and some soda bread to keep them going. It was Brid's idea. Deep down, my mother said, Brid was good hearted, thinking to pay her miserly aunt a call. But Titus always muttered about the farmhands. He told me Brid was the better looking then and according to his version it was the want of a husband that prompted the charitable visit.

They all said that the weather had been terrible. They had never seen rain like it before or since. The land was still soft and spongy from so much moisture. One of the stories my mother told me was of a terrible wet summer when people thought the sea was swallowing the land. Not a day went past throughout two weeks, and some said two months, that was not saturated.

Old people pummelled rosary beads and worried, but said nothing lest their families called them fools. And when it stopped they were scared to trust the new dryness as reeds and grasses hissed and the earth steamed. They were nervous to jab the fragile blue with sudden movement when the sky was so thin that a flock of birds might tear it. The elderly waited indoors and let the eager and the young test the day.

All her life my mother was solid and sturdy, but Brid was slight. In old photographs she looks wispy. She had dressed with special care that day. Titus always laughed over the attentions she once lavished on herself. The care she took of her appearance was legendary and for that walk she carried a pair of dainty sandals in her pocket and wore her plimsolls, while my mother strode out determinedly in stout walking boots.

Brid used to say that she was cut out for better things. She had her eye on the distance, dreaming of America. My mother said she would follow her. They were, until then, inseparable, great friends, always in the thick of things, according to uncle Titus. But to me they were always distant with each other, the remnants of sisterhood only present in their furious arguments.

As they approached the farm they saw their uncle's rick disappear and Liddy at the open door in her apron.

'Jesus! Get down!' Brid yelled to my mother who was standing, innocently to wave.

'Don't let her see us! We'll be called in to scrub the floor or worse. She'll have us worked to death before Uncle Jack comes back. I've me best clothes on, I'm not getting them ruined.'

The two bent their heads and crept off, continuing down the lane until the house was nothing but a smudge in the distance.

'We'll go up later, when Jack is back. Then she might give us tea.'

It was a fine day despite the previous weeks of rain. It was hot and the ground was drying out. They spread out their cardigans and lay back, watching the sky.

'I don't want to get covered in grass stains. What's my hair like, Mary?' Brid asked.

The O'Touney Sisters and the Day of Reckoning

My mother couldn't understand why her sister was so fussed. But Titus knew. There was a farmhand their uncle Jack said would go a long way. Titus would nod at me, but never say more. Once he told me he was the sort of fellow who saved up his money.

'He was what you might call sensible. A man with plans for himself.'

But my mother was unaware of their lives moving on, of futures that were to be decided. She thought then that her girlhood might last for ever.

That afternoon long ago they played. The ghosts of girls ran across the hills and cast shadows on the land, unaware of the darkest; the big soft bog at the bottom of the hollow.

Nestled between a crescent of slopes lay a treacherous patch of ground that was shifting and liquid. They ran down one of the slopes which turned into this and tumbled wildly, out of control, laughing. Brid was the first to sink.

As she felt herself drop she yelled to her sister to go back, but Mary could not stop and followed her straight in, up to the ankles.

Brid pulled her feet, but could not move them against the weight of earth, a great oppressive richness which held her fast. The heavy wetness pressed down as all around her the earth opened, to suck like a voracious mouth and close against her skin.

She flailed and thrashed, and sank further with each gesture of despair. Her calves were buried, but she would not stop struggling.

'Do something! Do something!' she shouted to her silent sister. Mary obediently began to scream.

They exhausted themselves with shouting. They yelled and howled, they pleaded, they begged. Their voices rang in that back of the way place where no one ever went. Marsh hoppers and dragon flies ignored them. A crow turned its head toward them, then looked away, and a solitary hare thrashed against the bracken on the outer ground before diving back into the darkness of leaves. It was hopeless. Brid wept as her legs disappeared. Around them insect life hummed and continued undisturbed. Mary began to pray.

Those Sailing Ships of His Boyhood Dreams

'Is that the best you can do?' Brid screamed as she struggled to push herself forward to the slope in the vain hope of catching at some long stems of grass.

'Prayers are useless. We need action, not words!'

Her voice was high and piercing and she continued to shout hoarsely as she moved with agonised slowness. Each effort caused her to sink further.

Mary remained rigid. She turned her face to heaven and the only movement from her was that of her lips mouthing an intercession to Saint Anthony, the patron of things lost.

Brid was desperate; swearing and yelling she continued to writhe and turn from the waist. She beat the surface of the bog with her fists, crying and wailing now that the soft ground had pulled her down as far as her thighs.

She knew that she was going to die. Shouldn't her life flash in front of her? Shouldn't she make her peace with God? And the sky was blue, it wasn't a day to die. Then she heard her sister shouting joyously.

'We're saved! We're saved! He'll get us out. Glory be to God, we're saved!'

'Where?' Brid shielded her eyes against the empty sky and saw nothing. Mary was fidgeting in her skirt pocket. Did she have a piece of rope or what?

Brid watched in amazement as her triumphant sister drew out her little capsule of Saint Anthony and held it up to heaven. The silver case flashed in the sunlight while Mary's lips moved in silent supplication.

'You omadhaun! Gombhean!' Brid was hysterical with impotent rage as the vision of her sister rose next to her, erect with her one hand towards the sky and her blue eyes lit by the sun, chanting the joyful mysteries.

'You great fool! This isn't Lourdes!' she screamed.

Brid knew that even if it had been, if they were sinking in some holy place, right in front of the altar and not in this god-forsaken spot away from everything, nothing would save them but their own wits. Even if they were to drown in the middle of the Vatican with the Pope looking on, all that could save them would be mortal intervention.

That was when she realised that the immortals were powerless.

The O'Touney Sisters and the Day of Reckoning

The sky was empty and only hands, solid and real hands, could haul them out. Prayers went nowhere, spent on empty air, just as their pleas for help had done.

And she knew the fault was theirs. They ought to have known the lay of the land, they ought to have recognised the signs, but earth disguises itself, even taking in farmers.

Buffer Kierney had lost a heifer in sinking soil, and once a commercial traveller passing through, parked his car in a field after a rainstorm while he warmed up in Dummican's lounge. He never saw it again.

Now Brid's waist was level with the ground. She wriggled like some crawling maggot. Mary felt her calves slip down further.

'Blessed Saint Anthony, help us in our hour of trial,' Mary prayed while Brid spat and cursed, and fought the land.

It was claiming them still living. Without decency the earth was opening into graves. It croaked its desire, without respect or dignity. Indecorously it held on while Brid twisted first one way and then the other in helpless rage.

Each move carried her further into the treacherous sinking soil. Soil that was water drenched where the sea lapped, where it seeped below the crust of earth they walked on every day without knowing. They were being pulled back to stay preserved with the forests and the tiny impressions of fossils, the print of a creature that had lived before the lands separated, before humankind stood upright. Down into ageless earth which nursed their past, hugged all of life to itself and to which they would surely return. They were being pulled down to lie along the unmarked famine graves, sinking to press upon the layers of battlefields, of warriors, of cattle raids and ritual burials. Sinking to add to the unwritten deeds, down among the carbon that was once part of the great wooden doorway, the massive square lintels, and the place where the storyteller sat.

But it was a bright, clear day; not a good one for taking a place in history. The two sisters held onto life with a desperation new to them and struggled against the promise they would one day keep with the earth. Brid fought a stern, material battle while Mary exhausted her soul with praying.

'Wait there!' a man's voice shouted.

Wasn't it one of the farmhands?

Those Sailing Ships of His Boyhood Dreams

'Praise be to God!' Brid yelled, her heresy forgotten. 'We're saved! We're saved!'

Tears poured down her face. Hysterical laughter bubbled in her chest. Already she had glimpsed the future. It was fate that brought them together in this desolate spot. Of all people to pass, but it should be that one. Him. She'd be making the crossing all right, herself and him together. She sobbed with relief.

Mary seemed unaware of anything, even danger was forgotten as she prayed. She continued her litany calmly while the farmhand backed the cart up and tied a length of rope behind. He threw this first to Brid who had sunk past her waist. She grabbed it and clung on as he slowly guided the horse.

The earth squelched, sucked and tore at her, then heaved its prize up ungracefully. Brid shrieked with fear as she felt herself come free. The rope dragged against her hands and the reeds cut her as she was pulled clear of the bog, up onto the slope.

She lay panting and shaking with fright. She had lost both shoes and her skirt, and was stinking of the brown mud, embarrassed in only her slip and blouse. She watched her sister who was by now up to her knees in the bog, but still upright and dignified, holding the silver capsule out.

They always said she must have looked like a saint in ecstasy and would laugh. It seemed that Mary had to be called twice before she heard her name. Then she too took the rope and later lay on the bank next to her sister. She had lost a shoe.

The young man was sweating from the exertion and the heat. Mud from the cartwheels had splattered him. Mary's legs were coated up to her knees with the stuff. She looked at them all and began to laugh, holding her skirt away so that it did not become further damaged. The hem was already ringed with brown. The farmhand began to laugh with relief. Brid cried and moaned as she attempted to straighten her slip over her legs, but it clung to them. Only the little silver capsule was untouched by earth, it alone shone clean and pure, while even the slope was cut into grooves from the wheels of the trailer, and the horse's flanks heaved and glistened.

Brid was unable to speak, or even look at the farmhand. Where she ought to have been grateful, she was only mortified, now that she was clear of danger. He must have seen her behaving like a

The O'Touney Sisters and the Day of Reckoning

madwoman, thrashing about and swearing. And now look at her, sitting in her slip like a great hussy, her face all tear streaked and mud everywhere. She had lost her best skirt. Then she remembered that her good sandals were in the pockets. There was no consoling her. She wailed all the way to the house.

They arrived at Liddy's sitting on the back of the cart. They waited outside while their aunt brought them kettles of hot water and they washed themselves out in the bit of yard at the back of the house. Their clothes were ruined. That was the day when mean Liddy Marnoch was forced to give them hospitality.

She brought out the oldest clothes she could find for them to wear. Brid sulked all afternoon in an old mac and a pair of her uncle's wellingtons, while Mary, her legs clean, went barefoot and prattled on about Saint Anthony with a shining face.

After washing, the farmhand cut huge slices of bread and made tea, and Liddy's eager eyes watched and counted each slice as it disappeared down the ravenous young gullets of Mary and their hired help.

Brid sat away from them, and had no appetitie. She said very little, just grunted in reply to questions. Her legs were cut and bleeding, great purple bruises were appearing.

All afternoon, they sat in Liddy's kitchen, drinking her tea and consuming entire loaves. Mary talked on happily and even Liddy had to laugh at the antics of the farmhand to amuse, as he waited on them, paying particular attention to Mary.

When he returned, the first thing their Uncle Jack did was to make the sign of the cross that they were both saved, but even he had to laugh at the way Mary recounted the story. He could tell already that it was destined to become one of the good tales for the dark nights: 'How Mary's faith remained unshaken'. But outside his house others told: 'How Liddy was forced to be generous'.

After that, Brid seemed to age quickly. She outgrew the young figure in the photographs. They must have soon become as dated as they are to me now. She was no longer the same laughing girl. It wasn't even that she changed so much physically, she always remained slim, but after that afternoon there was a tiredness about her. It was as if she had been worn away just as a wooden kneeler in church becomes indented with the shape of people's

Those Sailing Ships of His Boyhood Dreams

knees, and so retains the memory of prayers. Brid carried an impression with her from that day.

They said that it was as if some of Liddy's bitterness had rubbed off onto her. There's a saying about eating the bread of sourness. Brid, for all her lack of appetite, must have swallowed it that afternoon.

Everyone had a slightly different version of the story. They gave less importance to Saint Anthony of Padua, or more, according to their temperaments.

Of course my father always agreed with my mother, that Saint Anthony had saved the pair. Only he gave a different explanation of how the saint was effective.

'It was the light flashing on the case which blinded me that afternoon. So I turned back to see what it was.'

Uncle Titus always admired my father.

'He's a man who knows what he wants,' he would say to me every summer. 'You take a leaf out of his book, and you'll not do badly. He was always a man with plans.'

As a child I did not understand. I only knew that my mother was no sooner in the kitchen with my angry aunt, but the rows would begin. And that signified to me that the long school holidays had begun in earnest.

The Mermaid and the Rat Catcher

When the ratter stumbled out of the bar he was drunker than they all remembered seeing him and they were no strangers to the sight of Flanagan roaring drunk.

All day he pulled his body, dragging the dead half behind him and cursing the cruel god who had fashioned him this way. Bushmills killed the pain, so did Powers taken neat, and any Temperance Leaguers in the district knew to give him a wide berth. Even Father Malachy recognised a soul who'd suffered enough and gave him easy penance each time he came creeping into the dark world of the confessional with a hangover like a hatchet in his skull.

They were used to finding him sprawled wherever he'd dropped the night before; by the side of a track, at the bottom of a ditch, or in someone's barn. When he'd a gutful of the waters of life you'd have thought he was in the Grand Station Hotel, the way he slept.

Only with the whiskey burning a streak in his throat did his talk loosen and he would move bravely among men. In an argument his lifeless arm would shudder as he banged the table with his good fist or pointed for emphasis.

There were some college girls in the bar that night, down for the weekend to go sailing. So Sean the Driver and Gormley-Eyesight got him talking for sport.

'Here, c'mon and give us some of your crack,' they called.

Real men were inviting him into a world of golden glow and brotherliness. It was well known that Powers bought for you cut a better track than the one you bought yourself.

Gormley-Eyesight winked one bulbous look. 'Were you out at Lainard's the day?'

Suspicious and slow like an animal the ratter took the small glass held towards him. 'Aye,' he said, and with one tip of the head he emptied it. The drink warmed his chest. Sean the Driver got him another and Flanagan felt the heat of friendship pour away doubts.

'How many did ye get then?'

'Ah, Jasus, ten big bruisers.'

'Ten! Is that all?' Gormley-Eyesight opened his goitred eyes wide. They seemed to genuinely pop. He stared in two directions. The college-girls giggled.

'Jasus, they were the size of pups. Brown ones, black ones, chestnut backed, sleekit. They all came sniffing, with glossy fur, biting with their wild teeth.'

The ratter swallowed the ball of malt. Gormley-Eyesight bought him another.

'He's an ex-shpert.' He bowed theatrically to the girls and handed the glass over.

'Isn't that so? An ex-shpert in rodentology with diplomas from the University of Ballymun. That's right isn't it rat-man?'

Flanagan grunted and for a few seconds a twisted smile caught his mouth. But Sean the Driver became serious.

'There isn't anyone in these parts can touch him for knowledge though. No one at all, isn't that right?' he said, turning towards the ratter.

Flanagan was proud of his calling. He earned his own living and took no back-handers from anyone. And rats were intelligent. It was challenging work. They understood. He had to pit his wits against them with fierce cunning.

There was a scheme back in the forties when the council paid by the tail. He used to take them up in a sack and empty them on a table. Two men in overalls would count.

They kept him on, but wanted to give him some funny title, wanted him to do everything: bugs, fleas, lice, even rot in timber. They gave him a dark cap to wear and a quare sort of jacket that he couldn't button. He hung them up in the cloakroom by the pay office one Friday night and never put them on again. He went back to his first love.

Rats were smart, no one knew them like he did. He respected them and the animals sensed it. They understood why he had to kill them and he tried to be humane. He said rats were more compassionate than people because they did not bear grudges.

The Mermaid and the Rat Catcher

People told each other that he kept a couple as pets, but there was no harm in him they said, and left him alone.

Gormley-Eyesight mimed for the girls how they jumped over the cracks in the floor, because it was well known that Flanagan just let them run round his house.

'Wouldn't that be a sight now, two fine big rats sitting up waiting for you when you come home?'

Flanagan's home wasn't a real house. They all knew where he stayed. He lived out along the Lough Shore Road at the end of a footpath that was washed by mud in low tide and sank when the water line was high. That was where the timbered shed stood that had once housed the lobster pots of a family of long-gone fishermen, who chose instead to fish with bricks in America.

In the bar the girls giggled at Gormley-Eyesight's antics. Miniskirted, their dimpled knees twitched and he stared hard at the pink flesh. Sean the Driver felt the excitement of a foreign audience – three strangers who would laugh at the same worn stories they told every night.

'Tell them about the mermaids. He caught one you know. A big rat that was!' the Driver laughed.

'A mermaid?' one of the girls said. 'You're having us on.'

'I am not. Was I having you on about the rats? Hi, rat-man, tell these girls about that mermaid.'

Flanagan lurched forward, his breath soured with whiskey. He jabbed the air with his good hand.

'I did. I saw them. Two there were. A big one and a little thing, just out by the cove when I was going home.'

'Falling home, more like!' Gormley-Eyesight laughed.

The Driver whispered, 'Didn't they find him the next morning, wet through, down in the bay where the grey seals come in. I tell you, his head's cut. He's a wildman all right, out seeing mermaids when the rest of us are in our beds. Two bloody big aul' seals they were.'

But Flanagan was silent, remembering how he came to find them. Bright glittery things they were and he didn't care who believed him. No one could take away what he saw that night.

They were resting in that bit of the cove where, when the sea pulls back, the sand is always clammy even on hot days. He came limping over the pebbles with a dull head and bellyful of first rate poteen. Cursing the cold he headed for his one-roomed house. He insisted that it was a house – house enough for him without the added risk of falling down the stairs and no uphill climb to his bed each night. God the world was mad to keep building places the way they did. Seventy-five percent of injuries happen in the home. He'd seen a poster announcing that. Get rid of the stairs then, you'd halve the accident rate.

He started making his way up. He dropped from the high land to the smaller track that would bring him to his front door. Some days he carried a key. When he couldn't be bothered he hung it on the nail outside just so he could unlock the double doors and feel that he was master.

He thought then that he could see a light ahead. It looked as if someone was burning a candle on the beach. A pale gleam flickered. Maybe a weak torch beam. It glittered like a dying light, about to be extinguished, returning to the belly of darkness that let all creation bleed into the world, seeping out into the quiet places with the last, sad rays of anaemic day light.

Something stared out over the lough. A sea-monster. The hairs on Flanagan's arms stood out like a dog's. As he watched he saw the creature dip its head. It kept washing in the cold salt water that came in rivulets as if it was washing the earth bound traces off itself. Its movements were sudden and urgent. The ratter from that distance could sense the creature's fear. He thought that a wave must have carried it in before cruelly running back to the swell of the sea. The creature was left, wanting to return with it. Then he noticed that there was something else. Another being, smaller. A tiny thing. It looked darker. It was shiny. The familiar. He knew about such things. This was a sea-witch.

His foot slipped and the animal turned to stare at him. Its face was startlingly human, but paler than any living thing Flanagan had ever seen. It couldn't move away for it had no legs, instead, its lower half appeared to end in a great green sack. Its tail, he thought, of dry fish scales. 'A mermaid,' he whispered.

The creature was silent and continued to stare at him.

'If you're a mermaid I'll not harm ye,' he spoke up. He had started to lose his fear. What harm could the poor thing do him after all? 'I'll not hold you on dry land. Isn't that the death of the

The Mermaid and the Rat Catcher

likes of yous?'

The silent creature smiled. Its grin was wide, and rather coarse. Almost the same mocking look he was used to from the world of men. Then it spoke. It asked just to be left alone, said that it wanted to sleep before the sea returned for it. Its voice was quiet, but not what he'd call musical or anything special. He remembered how the mermaid lay back on the sand. He watched the outlines of its body.

He couldn't leave it. Not yet. Not without finding out more.

'What's that small thing with you?'

The creature covered it with its hand, and told him it was nothing but a small one. It floundered and tried to roll further away, pushing its familiar in front of it. It grabbed at its belly then seemed to clutch at its own green tail.

'It needs to be thrown back,' it said, and he thought that he would never forget this, as it showed him the familiar, and it had legs.

'It would never survive in the sea,' the creature said.

'Are you its mother?'

The creature stared out over the lough. When it spoke again it was just to tell Flanagan to leave. Its voice was brittle, and it told him to go away, begged him to continue whichever way he was going. But Flanagan wanted to know if it would come back. He would not budge. Finally it promised that at the next high it would swim down if it was a calm sea. And for this the ratter agreed never to tell a word of what he'd seen.

'They'll come out for me you see, they'll hunt me. Then I'll never be able to come back. I'd be destroyed by those men if you say anything to anyone.'

She sat back and watched him go, safe because he was that drunk he'd remember nothing. She sighed and gathered her energy for the last desperate act. She tugged the anorak tighter about her shaking legs. She was trembling and could not stop. She was losing blood. It left tell-tale traces on the sand. Her clothes were ruined. Crawling out as far as she could go she left the lifeless thing where the waves would steal it. It was her gift to the cruel sea. A peculiar kind of offering. Mary Mother, Star of the Sea, pray for the wanderer, pray for me. She spat into the bitter salt.

Those Sailing Ships of His Boyhood Dreams

The ratter knew that if he breathed a word then others would find the mermaids' secret places, would hide in them and destroy their fragile existence. He kept silent. But the creature did not return. He watched the shore, waited for calm tides. Counted the months. He had kept his word, and it broke its. Words that were written on water had no substance. He should have known. He had been tricked by a creature from the dissolving world. And he was angry.

Twelve miles down the coast in the next village it was rumoured that a baby had been caught up in a net along with the mackerel. But each fishing crew claimed that it had not been them. Maybe it was just a story after all. Their wives crossed themselves and prayed it was not some local girl, and the priest reminded them of the sanctity of family life each Sunday for a month.

Outside the hut Flanagan spent days howling. He writhed in pain, moaned about promises broken and hurled abuse at the sea. With his fists he beat the foaming waves of heavy tides. He alone raged on days when all around him the lough was calm. Then he got drunk. Then he spoke aloud. He broke the promise he made. Then he knew that it would never return.

'Tell them about your rats,' Gormley-Eyesight egged him on. And Flanagan told them how rats were more honourable than people, because unlike man, and every other creature, rats never broke trust.

When he stumbled out of the bar that night, he was drunker than anyone remembered seeing him and they were no strangers to the sight of Flanagan roaring drunk. Both Gormley-Eyesight and Sean the Driver reckoned they had got their money's worth from him for entertainment. They'd laughed to kill, watching the college-girls' faces. The antics of the man would keep them both going as they wandered home to waiting families, Sean to his wife and Gormley to his mother.

'Is that you son?' she'd say hearing his key in the door, like she did every night.

'Sure who else in the name of God would it be but myself?' he'd say bad naturedly, as was his custom. It was a funny old life at that, but there was room for all God's creatures in it. Room for his mother, room for the Flanagans of the world, but not too many of them, he chuckled, stumbling up the stairs.

'Are you all right out there, son?'

It was a calm sort of night. A soft darkness enveloped everything. It covered Flanagan, as it covered all things. And the ratter was alone. When he woke he was still out in the cove. That was as far as he'd reached. He was wet through. He didn't care. He chose to lie quite still. Someone coming on him might have thought that he was listening, the way a hunter listens for the sound of breathing. And if they had stepped closer they might have seen that his rheumy eyes were scanning the distance, watching for a deceitful, glittering tail.

Eiffel Tower

Frankie McDavitt was grateful to Samuel Beckett as she packed her rucksack one late May morning. She knew the letter she sent in response to the advert had been in good French, if her spoken skills lagged behind. Another summer spent in Paris would change that. Frankie was confident. Two summers ago she had scoured roadside cafes with a list of titles in her pocket after learning that the writer lived in the city. It was his French, and a holiday job, which first moved her to learn the language. But now her student days were over. She had to make a business arrangement.

She was engaged to teach English to a businessman's wife who wanted to be both cultured and hairless and spoke of language lessons and courses of electrolysis as a route to chic-ness. The terms were simple: in return for regular conversation, Frankie would be given board and lodging in Paris. She might even be able to take on further work. 'Suit a young graduate fine' the advert said. It suited Frankie McDavitt. A foot in the door of Europe, an opening up of the world after too many years of provinciality which three in Dublin could not quench.

Frankie packed apprehensively. She was worried about what people wore in Paris. They were all chic and weren't Parisian women supposed to be among the best dressed in the world? She remembered Paul once throwing out his hands with that shrug which spoke more than words.

'We put too much value on clothes,' he said. 'We decide whether someone is decent because of what they wear. I can relax here. Appearances are not so important, you all look so . . .' and he shrugged, summing them up in Dublin. On the industrial estate where his parents lived, he said, ordinary workers wore suits and had their hair cut at stylists. She thought how at home her mother wore wellingtons all the time, and only tied her hair back if she was going anywhere in the van. She used to cut their hair with the kitchen scissors.

'Leaving on Thursday?' the landlady said and began to write out a list of breakages for deductions from the deposit Frankie had given eight month before. Her room was bare; the huge wardrobe gaped, waiting for the next occupant to fill its cavernous mouth, long bored by a diet of Frankie's worn clothes and dirty washing in black bags between trips to the launderette.

Paul always polished his shoes; remembering this she began to polish the leather jacket. She rubbed saddle soap into the cracking, black leather, noticing how grey and scuffed the elbows were. The heavy zip was broken at the top. It was like that when Paul passed it on to her. She could never fasten it right up to the neck. Just as well it was summer, she could leave it open, hopefully her prospective employer would not notice.

The jacket was old, Paul told her that he had worn it for years, and when he bought it, it was second-hand. Now it was hers. Its red lining was split and frayed in places, and although she did her best to sew it up, the material was so worn that a needle entering it would have made the tear worse. She patched what she could and caught the sleeve lining back up. She had been meaning to do that for months. Every time she put the jacket on she caught the loose sleeve and the red arm would hang outside the leather, like a ribbon, or a flag. It drove her crazy.

She had nothing else. She could not even hope to be casual, because whatever she owned was falling to bits. She went to fetch her jeans from over the tin bath where she had hung them two nights before. They were stiff with soap. The water was never hot enough to wash it out properly. Even when she took them to the launderette they still looked grubby. She had soaked them overnight and scrubbed them with her nail brush. She folded them over, and they seemed to crack. They were bald in places. She lay them on the bed.

Paul could tell nationalities by the cut of the denim. He recognised Italians by the crotch hugging jeans they wore, Americans by the folds of extra material flapping. It was one of his maxims, 'you can always tell Americans by the arse of their trousers'. And Paul should know. He had left for America earlier that month. She couldn't remember if he had told her how the French wore theirs. But he was always neat, even when he described himself as being in his 'scruffy' phase, like Picasso in his blue period. Scruffy was a word she taught him. He liked it, and for a while he described everything that way, even her eyes.

She looked at the jacket as it lay across the chair in front of the dressing table. She used to study there by covering the mirror with newspaper so that she would not keep watching herself in the small room. The jacket looked neater; if it was not as good as new, it was as good as anything else she owned. She began to sort through the rest of her things. All her skirts were worn and tattered. Everything would need stitching. It was one of her ambitions to own clothes which did not fall apart. How would it feel to go to a drawer and take out whatever she needed, confident that she would not have to spend time repairing everything. She used to tell herself that one day, she would throw all her clothes out, and start again with things which were not disintegrating and would not split when she pulled them over her head. She would get smart.

She remembered that all the time she was a student she survived because people thought it was all right to be untidy. It was the fashion to look faded. But she saw the differences. Those who had good woollen jumpers when the days grew cold and warm coats which had not come from charity shops. And at graduation the same ones wore sober quality stuff. It seemed easy for them, the sudden formality. They laughed about parents who said they would not be ashamed of them, who took them shopping with open cheque books. Meanwhile she got the reputation for being eccentric.

But Paul understood. He waved his arm dismissively, he shrugged.

She worried as she packed. She had never seen her prospective employer. She did not want her to be put off at that first meeting.

When the Frenchwoman telephoned later that day, Frankie ran to take the call on the hall telephone. The front door of the house was open and a bus went past, so she did not catch what was said. The Frenchwoman spoke fast, making no allowance for Frankie's comprehension. Frankie was too nervous to ask her to repeat, in case the woman thought she was a fraud who spoke no French at

Those Sailing Ships of His Boyhood Dreams

all and had inveigled someone to write the letter for her. She quickly said several sentences of rusty French, as confidently as she could. Madame Despois arranged to meet her at Gare du Nord. She told Frankie that she was fair-haired, not very tall, and asked the girl what she would be wearing so that she might recognise her.

It was a cool day, yet when she returned to the room her palms were sweating.

When she next left her room she was carrying a small travelling bag containing a skirt borrowed from a friend, and a white cotton dress which Frankie's mother said could be taken anywhere as long as she remembered to wear an underskirt. The rest of her things she bundled up for the bin men. She wore the jeans and the leather jacket. She owned nothing.

After France she did not know. She would be twenty-two the day after tomorrow. She did not know what she was going to do with her life, she had no clear plan beyond wanting to get her French up to standard. Then she could try for other jobs. A secret dream of hers was to be bilingual. Just now she wanted out. It was the end of the spring in Dublin. She had worked a season in the pizza house. Still her mother wondered why she wouldn't come home, get a teaching job in the local school. Frankie would have suffocated, but her mother insisted that she was wasting her life in a filthy hole of a place, doing some half-cut job any Mary-Ellen could manage.

'You've qualifications. You could do anything,' she would complain, puzzled each time her daughter went home.

Do anything? So what? Frankie scoured newspapers for employment. Anything considered. She baby-sat, took dogs for walks, waited in pubs, served pizzas at two in the morning. She might as well go to New York and join the rest of her friends. Yet something stopped her. 'Europe' a voice whispered. 'See Europe first. There's plenty of time to end up in America. You'll most probably die in the new world, but for God's sake, see the old one first.'

She was doing the journey in two overnight crossings. It worked out cheaper to travel the length of England during the day, from Liverpool where she would arrive early the first morning. She would get to Paris after two nights of no sleep. What would she look like for that first meeting? Hardly her best.

She had sorted out books that would be useful as study aids and planned a list of conversation topics. She bought a file from the student's union shop and collected news items, anything of general interest that she could use for teaching. On the train out of Connolly Station she went through the material nervously, hoping that she would give the impression of being a well organised teacher.

It was a long gruelling journey, and uneventful much of the way. She read and tried to sleep. The lounge was stuffy. Although it was still night, several of the passengers got sick and early morning Liverpool had a smell of stale vomit that she could not shake as she wandered up to Lime Street for the connecting train. There was a green bus, but people were pushing and shoving so she decided to walk the distance. It was a route she knew by heart from the summers spent as a student, crossing to work in London.

At Folkestone harbour that evening, she walked up the gangplank once they had been instructed to board. There was always so much waiting around on journeys, sitting in this rest room or that waiting area, that she could not remember where she had passed most of the day until then. She left her bag in the hold as the deck hands shouted at them to leave everything, but she clutched the cardboard file to her.

The boat was smaller than the Dublin boat and completely different inside. There were better lounges and deck areas. It had a holiday feel about it, unlike the Irish boats. They were definitely working vessels, sending migrants out. The journeys on them felt final, most of the people on board were saying goodbye to someone, but this boat had the quick feel of a bright thing returning, suntanned and clutching a postcard.

Her stomach felt empty. She had not eaten since morning, but really did not want to break into what money she had. She walked around. The boat was crowded and she looked everywhere for somewhere to sit. All the places seemed to be occupied, bags had been left on empty seats, reserving them, and some people were already stretched out for the night across the floor of the lounge. All the pullmans were taken, and the only free places she saw were in the bar, so she made her way back there and sat down by a table.

Those Sailing Ships of His Boyhood Dreams

Instantly the person sitting opposite began to talk. It was as if they had been waiting for someone to occupy that chair so they could begin a conversation. She did not blame them for wanting to divert the dreary hours of the journey, only she was not settled in and it felt strange the way the questions began abruptly.

'Where is your destination?' they asked, and 'Are you staying long there?'

She looked up. The speaker was a thin, dark-haired man who appeared to be swamped by upholstery. He receded into the chair as if he was losing a battle of assertion over furniture. His voice was not loud, and at first it shook a little. He coughed several times to clear his throat. Although he asked the basic questions which any traveller might, Frankie realised that he was not at all curious about her, because he hardly waited for answers. Rather he was eager to speak himself and to tell anyone who would listen the sole fact that he was travelling to Nice.

'Nice,' he repeated, rolling the name around his tongue as if he could taste it.

'How nice,' Frankie said and immediately had to bite her cheek.

'Yes, yes,' he continued, rubbing his hands together in anticipation. 'I will spend the entire summer there, away from everything. I will read, and paint, and think.'

He sat back in his chair and put his finger tips together. At first she thought that he was merely thinking aloud until she saw him looking at her, waiting for agreement.

'I am not one of those people who spend their holidays lazing in the sun along a beach somewhere. Oh no,' he continued. 'I have to keep using this.' He pointed to his forehead.

'Yes' Frankie said, feeling uncomfortable. She felt that he wanted her to approve.

She tried to sink back into the yellow upholstery. She could not get comfortable. There was no way she could stretch out in the chair. Designed to make certain no one overstayed their time at the bar, it was rigid and inflexible. There was no way she could put her head back, and the arm rests were too narrow. She tried every position she could, and finally, defeated, sat upright. The man was watching her. As she caught his eyes he began to talk.

'This is my annual holiday,' he said. 'All year I work, and every summer, for six weeks I escape.'

She smiled politely. She did not care what he was escaping. She had spent all day travelling and wanted to put her head back and doze, and it was impossible. She felt disgruntled and irritable. She knew that the lights in the bar never went out. All over the boat people were settling in for the night and she was stuck. She decided she would get a drink. To hell with the expense. She put the folder on her seat to mark it. That was one of the perils of travelling alone. If she left her coffee on a counter while she went to go to the toilet, when she came back her place could be gone, her coffee cleared away by over-zealous staff.

'Would you mind my place?' she asked and the man nodded so effusively, and said so many times that it was 'no trouble' and 'not at all' and that he was 'glad to oblige' that she wished she had said nothing.

The bar was packed. She walked around trying to find the thinnest place in the crush. When she caught the bartender's eye he served her warm flat Guinness in a plastic cup. People were pushing for this? It tasted bitter. She could not finish it but left it on a ledge and went outside.

The deck was full of people staring out to sea. Couples starting their holidays held hands and laughed. By the door a man and woman were carrying on unashamedly while others, more discreet, cuddled along the wooden benches. Not for the first time Frankie wished Paul had not left for America.

She stood leaning over the rails, watching the boat move away. The sea looked terribly cold. She stared at the lights around the harbour and watched their reflection until they vanished. The boat gathered speed. Already land was vanishing from view, receding into the dark which came down suddenly. The boat cut channels, and the grey foam was angry and spiteful as it pulled away.

Night crossings are lonely. This is when the desperate choose to jump, and who would notice? The dark wetness covers the head like another birth, re-entering that slumbering state. And water can be very still. Inland lakes and canals have smooth surfaces. Once, when walking round a pond at dusk, Frankie panicked as the soft light vanished into evening. She kept walking until the pond was safely behind her but could not stop shaking.

Water is the cruellest element. It lets you imagine that you are in control, snapping back just as it has lulled you into comfort.

Those Sailing Ships of His Boyhood Dreams

Then it shows you who really holds the rein.

She leant on the rails, letting the wind tug at her hair, whipping it across her face. Frankie laughed for the first time since setting out as she caught loose strands back with one hand. She stared at the sky. The stars were beginning to appear. There was no mark between earth and air. All joined together into an infinite darkness, through which the boat moved on this sleepless night. A speck of humanity, surrounded by nature in its cruellest form.

If she was afraid of anything she thought that it was of drowning; of being far from land, far from everyone, descending into the receiving sea. She imagined her hand reaching out to touch only more water, fingers flailing. She knew that it would be soundless, as it sucked her down. Once she had dreamt that water was death. It flowed inside the eye hollows of the skull and tinkled against its white ribs. And she heard its threat whispered as a child. The breathing sea was silent and terrible, and it would wait, pulsing like a severed vein.

A girl she had been at school with once told her how she had attempted to cut her wrists. She had placed them under running tap water because she'd heard that this way you did not feel it. Frankie imagined those taps swirling blood down the bath, into the sewers and out into this same sea. And there were still suicides bleeding uselessly into it, their desperate shouts for help watery and faint, while others were salvaged from brine-encrusted death.

All around Frankie the sea ebbed then poured back in one great swell of despair. She had felt barnacles and the tight green grip of sea ribbon as it wrapped about her ankles. She had seen tides carry fronds and branches broken from their holds and push brown gelatinous weeds towards the shore, beaching the quivering jellyfish before drawing away. The sea deserts even its own but returns like a torturer to prolong that state called dying.

They said that drowning was peaceful. She thought it must be the worst kind of end. Better to cut your wrists and have done with it. Her friend had fainted and come round the next morning in the cold bathroom of an empty house. The cuts congealed at the base of her hands. Cuts which were only surface, the razor blade too painful, the water useless.

No one paid her any attention. She was back at work the next week. 'Do it properly next time,' one of her brothers said. So she did, choosing this time a quiet inland lake.

Frankie's mother had written to her after the body was found, slipping it into the letter to drown between lines about the price of grain and a field of cabbage spoiled by the early frost. Do you know who's dead now? The colour of her aunt's new jacket, and was she coming home at all? Only they'd have to air the mattress, so could she let them know?

She felt cold and went back inside, grateful for the lights and noises in the bar.

'Did you have a walk around the deck? Is it very windy up there?'

She heard the questions as soon as she sat down. She had forgotten the little man. Now he sat forward in his chair, eager and bright, his eyes inquisitive, like a child's.

'I might go up later. Freshen me up a bit, blow away the cobwebs. I'm not afraid to pit myself against the elements. Not like some people. I'm not one of these who have to stay inside when its raining, Oh no. Life's rich tapestry. That's what artists need to be part of.'

She did not look at him. 'It's very cold, I'd take your coat.' She hoped he would go for a walk.

'Ireland!' he said and pointed at her with the triumphant smile of an invalid who has finished a jigsaw puzzle.

Frankie looked down at her chest to where he pointed, imagining a map had suddenly appeared across her jersey.

'The land of the singer and the poet,' he told her. 'And which are you?'

'The unemployed.'

He did not go out on deck. He stayed and told her his life story. She asked no questions yet he made her feel as if she was interviewing him. She nodded. He taught in a primary school. He called the children his colleagues.

'I can relate better to the children than the adults in that place,' he said. He was desperate to talk. She wondered if there was no one interested enough to listen to him back there, so now he had to trap a stranger.

He talked endlessly about himself. The middle son in a family where all the children were expected to do well.

Those Sailing Ships of His Boyhood Dreams

'Both my brothers are doctors, like my father. I'm the odd one. Teaching in a primary school. I wanted to be an artist.' He spread out the palms of his hands with a gesture that accepted his defeat. 'I'm not what you'd call a great success.'

He stiffened his back and seemed to speak mostly to himself, for his voice was low and quiet. He mumbled that he was a person of many interests.

'I have my passions, my concerns. I have never stopped learning, just because I was not one to do well at school, I've made up for it with the rest of my life. Did evening classes. I was going to sit exams but it all got too much for me, with working during the day, but I followed the open university course. Art history is my specialism. That's why I'm going to France.' He looked at her, his face brightening as he got into his stride.

'Of course, the language is no problem for me. Such a beautiful language, such a wealth of literature, Balzac, Molière, Flaubert. This holiday I will read and read. That's what I do best.'

Frankie watched people walking back from the bar. She wondered whether they would close it, cranking down the rolling metal curtain. Behind that the crew could continue to drink. It was a strange life, being a ferry worker. A girl back home had worked the Dublin boats one season. She met her in Liverpool, of all places. Pam was there for a day before sailing that night.

'Don't you get confused?' Frankie asked her. She thought that she would forget which place she was in. Pam said she was going to stick it out.

'When I've got my sea legs, I can go deep sea, so I've got to clock up the time. I'll be off then all right. Japan, Australia.'

It was Pam who told her about the after-sessions drinking and the carry-on below deck. She did not feel confident about boats after that.

She heard him telling her that he made puppets with the children and at the end of each year would let them put on a show. That was his achievement, but he loathed it.

'I wanted to design sets for the theatre.' His face looked sad, but he brightened. 'For an entire summer I escape, at least,' he grinned.

Frankie wondered what from, but could not have asked him. She could not take him seriously. He continued talking like one desperate to persuade a judge that he is a responsible, valuable member of society and can be let out alone.

'I'm shy usually, but once a year, on holiday, I let go,' he grinned.

She noticed that he was drinking out of a brandy glass, and the tiny hand which gripped the stem was like a doll's. When he stood up, he was short, his frame no bigger than a young boy's, his dark beard a trick on a hairless face.

At one point she went to the purser's desk; his relief when she returned was so transparent that she felt it necessary to reassure him.

'I just had to check something,' she said, feeling awkward and protective.

All night he talked about writers he had read, about places he had been. If it was a conceit it was an odd one because he measured his inconsequence against these. Frankie saw how he chipped away at the image he wanted, each time he spoke.

They were both taking the train to Paris. His connection to Nice was not until the evening. He had asked her what he ought to see in one day and she said he could try to see the Impressionist paintings, or just walk along the Seine. She told him how to get to the Left Bank, and to Notre-Dame. He wrote directions down in a small blue notebook.

'I always carry a notebook, for any ideas I have. I like to be prepared. Sometimes, I write poetry.'

That was the point when Frankie fell asleep before he had the chance to suggest that she might like to hear some of it.

Instructions came over the tannoy. The boat was docking at last. He became agitated. His speech slurred, and when the call came to disembark, he seemed to slip. She caught him, and he must have thought he could rely on her because he kept close by and she found herself accompanying him to get their luggage. He had an enormous rucksack. She had to help him put it on. He could not manage the straps. She realised that he was drunk.

'It's so heavy,' she said seeing how it dwarfed him.

'Oh, it's full of books and paints,' he told her quickly, as if she had accused him of a crime.

'I intend to work,' he said, drawing himself up. 'I'm not one of these that lie around in the sun.'

'Yes, you told me.'

He smiled sloppily as if she had awarded him a mark of distinction.

She had slept, despite the lights in the bar, a terrible, unsettled sleep. Whenever she opened her eyes, she saw him clutching a glass, watching her. He must have drunk cognac after cognac. He staggered on the gangplank, laughing stupidly at nothing. At the control desk she had to help him find his passport.

On the train she threw her bag up onto the rack and sat down in a window seat. She stared out but the glass reflected the carriage as in a mirror. He was behind her like a terrible painting that has hung for so long in the same place that no one notices it until it's removed. She prayed that other people might join the carriage. At last an elderly Frenchwoman did. They began to chat. The woman told Frankie that she had to meet her daughter-in-law who had recently had a baby. Her son, the father, 'he's in the police force,' was currently in hospital.

'Just after the birth,' she said, shaking her square head, 'he fainted in the excitement. The imbecile hit his head on the metal leg of the bed. The mother comes out with the baby, and the father? He's kept in. Twelve stitches. It's more than they gave her.'

They laughed together, but the little man looked perplexed and was silent. He avoided looking at the woman and leaned across to tell Frankie that she spoke what he considered to be good French.

'Yes,' he told her, 'your French is certainly up to a high standard from what I have heard.'

Frankie had to stop herself from asking for a tick, like he would mark in a child's exercise book.

'You have obviously studied it in some depth.' His voice cut into her private world again, like an intruder.

'Did you study at university??'

'Not French,' she replied with a bad grace. 'Languages are not my subject.' Frankie wondered for a moment whether she should tell him, just to shut him up, that she used to fuck a beautiful French man. 'I did it at school.'

'I suppose you had coaching?' His eyes were beady.

She remembered an old nun once saying to a girl in her form, 'Frankly Anjelica, you are so slow, the only way you can hope to succeed in any subject would be to have constant coaching outside school.'

'Of course not,' she told him.

That hurt. Let him be the reader, the poet, the thinker. A nice comfortable existence. Another place and she might have despised him for it, yet he was such a casualty.

There was a time when Frankie thought that she might become an artist. She kept very quiet about it, told no one for fear of being laughed at. She could not have played at being an artist. Once, a young man in the same tutorial group as her, saw some sketches she had made. He said that they were as good as anything he might do, in fact, he did not think he could produce a higher standard than the one she, and thus he, had already reached. Such praise indeed! She called him a self-centred half-brain, and he was surprised at her anger. Now she sat in the carriage shaking with self control, hearing another voice in her head: 'Your French is certainly up to a high standard.'

She stared out of the window, but all she could see was her own face. She was angry and she breathed slowly. She did not want to have to listen to him, but he was brave now, with cognac. Talking like a man, or so he thought. Suddenly he leant against her in the carriage. She told him to lean away, and he giggled nervously.

She supposed that she slept, because she could not remember the woman leaving. She heard whistles blow as the train made various stops, but not much else until around 5 a.m. when she knew there was no point trying to sleep any more. As soon as she sat up, he was there, telling her that he had a whole day to spend in Paris. Outside it was grey and cold and he had slept off his cognac.

'What are you going to do?' he asked her. When she told him that she was going to meet an employer that morning, he seemed surprised that she was not on holiday. But he quickly recovered himself and asked if she would meet him for lunch.

'Only I've got a whole day in Paris, to walk around.' He sounded panicky.

Frankie explained that she had no idea where she was going to be, and so could not possibly arrange to meet him. And then the strangest thing happened, his face crumpled, right in front of her. She thought he might cry. She could not help staring.

Those Sailing Ships of His Boyhood Dreams

'A whole day in Paris,' he said. His voice shook. 'And I really hate walking around places on my own.'

She had never seen anyone look so scared. He had six weeks to escape, six weeks to be alone, to be an adult, to be the person he thought he ought to be.

'Look,' she said, 'I'm meeting my employer this morning, and I'm anxious to go.'

He nodded. Frankie didn't know what made her do it, but she heard herself saying that if she could manage it, she would meet him.

'Under the Eiffel Tower then?' he said, seizing the chance she held out. 'Because I thought that's what I would like to see, so I'll be there anyway. At two o'clock, if you can make it?'

She nodded. The poor man. Under the Eiffel Tower. Frankie wanted to laugh. He had no idea, suggesting that. Four pillars named after the compass points and hundreds of people around them. You could search all day and never know who was there.

The Eiffel Tower, scene of so many suicides, waiting for the adventurous and the foolhardy. The crudest of picture postcards pinned up on a board. To Frankie it was an uncomfortable sight. The towering spirals of networked steel, the engineering to produce vertigo. It was a scene of nightmares.

The Eiffel Tower, desperate fingers claw at its sides, hanging on for survival. An awful monument to the bodies thrown from it.

'I can't come to Paris and not see the Eiffel Tower,' he said grinning. 'If you can make it, just turn up.'

Again she nodded.

It was a clear, cold morning as the train arrived in Paris, thawing into late day. Tired and groggy she could only stumble and wait.

From the Eiffel Tower, visitors to the city watched the sky clear and felt the first warm rays of the sun. They saw the roof of the Gare du Nord, the Tuileries, Notre-Dame. They saw the terrible confluence of roads around the Concorde, saw Sacre Coeur, white-domed in the distance. Under the Tower the ant-like processions of people marched, shadowed by its fretwork. Frankie wondered if anyone saw the man whose face crumbled as he walked, afraid to be alone. Did some turn to watch him wait?

By two o'clock she was in another arrondissement, making

Eiffel Tower

arrangements and drawing up a time-table of hours, being shown a new neighbourhood. They stopped for lunch before driving out to where she would live. They toasted their agreements and Madame Despois paid the bill. Through the bottom of her glass Frankie watched the Tower, so tiny it fitted inside her brandy. She could drink it in one gulp, swallow its terrible menace. Under it, she knew he must have waited, feeling lost among so many. If she could have run there, she would have, just to shout to him so that he would not be alone. Frankie's only consolation was that in the crowd he would never know if she was there or not.

The small man stepped onto the pavement. He walked some distance then stopped and read the street signs. He had all day to drink in the city, only one day. There were vast treasure houses of art here, but he would not stop. Big places terrified him. He was to spend the summer in a villa owned by one of his aunts. Safe. He thought he might come back to Paris on his way through, try and see the Louvre. Would a day do it? Yes, he was sure that would be enough, then he would have seen the place. But he could manage a night here surely? He could walk the streets and find an hotel. Others did. They told him about their summers when they returned in the autumn. He always went to Nice. He could say that he met a woman on the boat, and let them draw their own conclusions. After all, he had asked her out, in a roundabout half-baked sort of way, but he had done it. And her face had not turned away from him, had not turned up in disgust, had not broken into laughter. No, her face had remained blank. But she had explained how she was fixed. That was fair. He decided to follow the rue Saint Denis and as he walked off he stood a little taller, as if he was pulling himself up from the heels. He was almost jaunty as he disappeared into the road whistling.

The Faithful Departed

Clothilde was vague about times and dates. She forgot birthdays, family events escaped her, she even forgot her children's names. But that was not surprising. She had so many in a rush. All she did when she was first married was push out babies, sweat through miscarriages, and change nappies.

Her first husband died. Walking home drunk one night, he fell into the canal, leaving her alone with five children.

Her mother told her straight, 'A woman needs a man's wage packet.'

She had no option but to remarry and so the cycle of birth continued without a break, until her body stopped of its own accord. By the time she was forty-five her hair was white, she walked with a stoop, and forgot things.

But there was one date she never forgot, May 14th 1937. She even knew that it had been a Friday. That was the day, fifty years ago, when her sister took the steam train as part of the works outing. A weekend in London, capital of the Empire.

Clothilde could still see Hilda as she looked then. She was laughing, wearing her battered cloche hat. She mounted the first step of the train worrying that they would have to travel back in the dark. She was nervous, it was a journey of a lifetime. They were to have breakfast and lunch en route in the dining wagonette. It took the best part of a day to travel down from the north of England then.

Hilda was the tallest of Clothilde's three sisters. Agatha and Miriam were both departed. She could not remember the dates of their deaths but she knew they were alive then; they all went to wave Hilda off. Nothing was ever as significant again as that Friday, May 14th 1937.

Hilda was very slim, always was. As a child she got called skinnymalink. It made her cry. She got over it. She looked fine

Those Sailing Ships of His Boyhood Dreams

that day in her grey two-piece. It was not her best, but it suited her.

Clothilde remembered how the steam obscured her as the train stoked up. A blast of grey smoke covered Hilda's ankles, rose up across her face as she stood on the steps, neither in nor out the train.

The porter came down the line slamming doors and Hilda skipped up into the carriage. She cranked the handle to lower the window and hang out. The station master blew his whistle and there followed the loudest noise any of them had ever heard as the train started. They clapped their hands over their ears in fright. The steam cleared and they saw Hilda waving. She looked terrified. Clothilde was certain that had she been able to open the door, she would have jumped off, right then.

When Sunday night came, there was no sign of Hilda.

She was married to someone, a Frank or a Fred, and he turned up at their house. He stood out in the street and asked them if their clock was right and would they mind checking.

'My pocket watch has gone barmy,' he said, pressing it to his ear.

An hour later he went to the police station and described her.

Miriam ran round to a girl Hilda worked with, and was told there was no works trip.

'Hilda didn't come in for work on Friday. She told us she was going to London because a rich relative had died and she was called down to hear the reading of the will. She said he was a toff.'

Miriam stood in the hallway and the girl's father shouted at them to either get in, or get out.

'Make your minds up. It's bloody freezing with that door open.'

'It's Hilda Braithwaite, Dad. She's disappeared.'

He came to the door pulling his braces over his vest.

'Eh lass, you'll have to go to the police.'

But Hilda's husband had already been there.

'What did they tell you?' their mother asked.

He would not come in but stood outside under the street lamp. The light made him look sick.

'They don't know anything,' he said. 'She's not even a missing person until Tuesday.' He shrugged, disgusted.

The Faithful Departed

They stood outside in silence. It was foggy, and their mother was coughing.

'Well we can't stop here all night,' Agatha said, but no one moved.

He stared up the street.

'She always was a bloody liar,' he said. Then he turned and walked home.

Clothilde stood in the queue at the post office, clutching her pension book to her chest. She was winded after a life of work, rush and worry, without time to look around, or pause for breath.

She could not remember her age exactly but sixty-eight felt like a good approximate. Hilda was four years older. When she caught that train she must have been about twenty-two.

Although they were all worried that night, they expected there was a reasonable explanation. Some mix-up and poor Hilda stuck out in London, having missed her train.

'You know,' their mother said, 'she was worried about travelling in the dark. I mean, those drivers can't see where they're going can they?'

Hilda's husband came round again on Monday. He had been up to her workplace and was told that she had asked for her cards on Thursday.

They began to feel suspicious when he said that her best hat and shoes had gone as well.

'Now that's what I call sly,' he said. 'Going out in her old things so I wouldn't notice. All the time I kept telling her, "Take your new hat. You might as well dress up, all the rest will," and didn't she swing me some line about not wanting to get the hat ruined, in case it rained and wanting to wear her old shoes because she'd be walking round all day.'

He was more angry at being taken in than worried that his wife had disappeared. He kept discovering other things missing. On Tuesday he came round.

'Her costume jewellery has gone. She never intended coming back did she?'

They stood at the door with their arms folded, feeling angry. None of them had been in on the secret. Soon the whole street would know.

Those Sailing Ships of His Boyhood Dreams

It had been a well planned escape.

'I reckon we should have known something was up,' they all said later.

'We haven't seen your Hilda about in months,' neighbours said at Christmas. And once a year after that, during the festive season, Agatha would stand up, throw out her arms for silence and begin:

'Even as she waved to us at the station, she knew that she would not be coming home. Never again would we see her face, never again would we hear her voice. Gone! Gone! A last goodbye.'

It became a popular recitation, and Agatha was in great demand for parties. Their mother always used to say if you could play the accordion, you'd never be lonely during the public holidays.

But Clothilde knew something the others didn't. The week before her sister took the train to London, she came round to her mother's house. Clothilde was in on her own, Hilda asked her to mind a bag for her, not a particularly good one, but she told her she had bought it recently and did not want him to go mad about her spending money. Hilda was always in debt, and would have borrowed off Clothilde if she had any to spare.

'Don't show anyone,' she told her. 'Not Mam, not anyone.'

So Clothilde stuffed the bag in the bottom of the wardrobe and said nothing.

When Hilda called round to collect it the next day, she wanted Clothilde to bring it out to the yard so she could nip back home down the entry.

But their mother was sitting in the kitchen, eating a boiled egg without her teeth in.

'How long is she going to be?' Hilda was furious. 'I can't wait outside all day. Stick it under your coat.'

But Clothilde wasn't wearing a coat. She couldn't understand what all the secrecy was about, but she went upstairs to fetch the bag from the wardrobe.

It was an ordinary, black leather handbag, a bit larger than something she might choose for herself, but unremarkable in every way. It was still stuffed with paper, the tissue they pack things with in stores. Hilda must have been in such a hurry to hide the bag she hadn't emptied it out. If that was what being married did, had you creeping round like a shadow, hiding things, she'd think twice before she walked up the aisle.

She reached back into the wardrobe to pull out a jacket, and as she leaned over she tripped on the turned up end of lino, where the edges did not overlap properly. The bag fell from her hand, and as it hit the floor it burst open. Bundles of pound notes sprang everywhere.

'Jesus, Mary and Joseph!' Clothilde whispered. There was more money than she had ever seen in her life. She went down on her knees stuffing the bundles back inside the bag.

'Oh God, if anyone walks in on me, what will they think I'm doing!'

There was more money than she could earn in a lifetime. She packed the green bundles deep into the bag. She started to shake.

What was her sister getting involved in? How had she got this money? All sorts of notions rushed through her mind. No one earned that kind of amount honestly.

In the yard she was jumpy. Hilda asked her immediately, 'Did you look inside?'

Clothilde shook her head wildly. She wanted to pass the bag back and forget everything. Maybe Hilda had borrowed the money.

She had an unorthodox way of securing a loan. What she could not borrow, she took: rent money, club money, change for the window cleaner and the bread man, all went missing. Of course, Hilda always intended to return it. And she always told the person she had taken the money from, with a peculiar, but compelling honesty after the stealth of the event.

Now she had enough to retire on.

Clothilde decided to speak to her, when the house was empty.

Hilda took the bag from her and put it under her arm.

'I'd get that jacket back before Mam gets suspicious,' she said. 'You can pretend you were letting me try it on.'

Upstairs Clothilde hung it back inside the wardrobe. She was frightened.

'If she asks me to mind anything again, she's got another thing coming.'

She was about to leave the room when her eye noticed something. One of the bundles must have rolled away on the lino. It was caught up under a crack. Clothilde could hear her pulse race.

Those Sailing Ships of His Boyhood Dreams

She stared, then lurched and seized the roll. Tearing at the band of paper that bound it, she flattened the notes out and divided them into two amounts, which she stuffed inside her shoes. She was sweating. She walked with difficulty.

'Are you getting into bed with your shoes on?' Miriam asked her later that night as they prepared for sleep. She could not kick them off until the light was out She tried moving some of the money when she went to the lavatory, but her skirt and blouse had no pockets, and she could hardly go out to the yard carrying a handbag. Her sisters knew when it was her time of the month, and they'd look at her soft.

'No, it's a bit cold, the lino, on bare feet, I'll switch the light off,' she said and she waited by the wall switch.

Usually they raced each other to bed because whoever was last had to cross the floor and put out the light.

'Can you hear rustling?' Agatha said as they lay in the dark. 'Like something walking over paper?'

Miriam sat up, pulling the sheets around her – she was terrified of mice, and someone had seen rats in one of the yards only a few days before.

'Oh God! You don't think we've got rats,' she wailed.

They called Clothilde, but she was rigid in the bed, pound notes crunched inside her palms. She didn't reply.

She lay without moving while her arms ached with cramp. Only when she thought both sisters were asleep did she stuff the remaining money in her pillow case.

She thought Hilda would come round and ask her what was going on as soon as she discovered a roll was missing. Then Clothilde would pull the notes out and ask her what she had been up to. She could not let anyone know about this because it would worry her mother to death. But she would get the truth out of Hilda if it killed her.

Hilda was not fond of the truth, it was too simple, too dull. Not that she was a liar, but her imagination was certainly lively.

Once she ran away from home. A couple found her and took her to the police station, concerned that the young girl needed protection. Hilda had kept them entertained with stories about her wicked step-mother who threw her out at night and bolted the door against her.

After that their father would lock the bedroom door. Hilda became very good at escaping. Once she tied bed sheets together and climbed from the second-storey window to the street, carrying her heeled shoes in her mouth, by the ankle straps, so as not to ruin them.

Clothilde, who shared the bed with her then, woke frozen with cold, because all the covers had gone. Even the curtains had been twisted round in a rope. None of the sisters had heard anything.

Hilda crept home early the next morning, but her father was ready and he took his belt off to her. He had been sitting up all night and was half mad. She screamed, louder than was necessary they all thought, but she wanted the neighbours to know.

That morning when the knocker-up came he did not need his pole, every window was open, people were arguing and yelling. The entire street had erupted.

'Stop that bloody racket!'

'Lay off her, I've heard about you!'

'You've been listening to stories then, haven't you? What's she been saying this time?'

Her inventiveness always amazed them.

But Hilda did not come round for the missing money the next day She did not mention it, even when they went to see her off. Clothilde wondered if Hilda knew what was in the bag, maybe she had been so busy that she had not discovered the loss. She tried to work up courage to pull her aside and ask her about it, but she could not get her away from Miriam and Agatha.

Long after Hilda vanished, Clothilde kept quiet. It was as if Hilda was buying her silence, and she was corruptible.

Somehow, after that, Clothilde forgot about it, and forgot about the bag. Somehow, the secret hoard was used up. She bought a good coat and told them she had saved up. She tore off the price ticket before she brought it home. For the first time in her life she had proper underthings, not cast-offs.

Some of the mystery was solved when it was discovered that a young man in the machine shop had left work about the same time as Hilda.

'Who the hell is he?' their father asked, but no one knew him well. He was not local, and the only thing people could recommend about him was that he was good on the horses. He was always in the bookies during dinner break, sometimes winning, most times losing. Hilda had become friendly with him. The family assumed that they had gone together. Clothilde knew that the money must have come from a win.

Life was quieter without Hilda. There used to be endless squabbles about clothes and jewellery. Even after she had married and gone to live with whatever he called himself, she would still come around to see what clothes she might borrow.

Clothilde remembered coming home from a friend's house one night. She saw her sister on the other side of the street, very smart in a new green jacket and matching hat. Suddenly Agatha appeared from nowhere, screaming and dragging things off her.

'They're mine! They're mine!' she yelled. 'Give them back, thief!'

But Hilda refused to take the things off.

In full view of everyone they started tugging and pulling. They had the jacket between them, Agatha siezed a sleeve and yanked it behind Hilda's back. Clothilde heard the terrible rip as the lining went. Agatha shrieked as if she had been wounded.

'Eight weeks I saved up for that!'

Hilda stepped out of the jacket neatly. It fell onto the pavement. She looked at it with disdain.

'Have it. It's in the gutter. That ought to make you feel comfortable. You belong together.'

Agatha flew at her.

'Give me back my bloody hat, you bitch!'

She tore at Hilda's head. Hat pins came away with handfuls of hair. Hilda shrieked.

'Look what you've done!'

'I'll do more than that,' Agatha shouted, rolling up her sleeves and looking mean.

Hilda gave her sister a withering look and turned on her heel. She continued down the street, hatless, jacketless.

Agatha screamed abuse. Tears poured down her face. Hilda turned the corner with all the assurance of knowing that she at least had behaved like a lady.

Clothilde collected her pension from the post office, and counted.

The Faithful Departed

Inflation. Forty pounds used to be a fortune. Now it was nothing. But she had woken up with a feeling that this was the day of all days. She had to go. She had let fifty years slip away, God knows, she might not last much longer.

At the ticket office she paid for the shoppers' special day return to London. It was an off peak bargain. She put the ticket carefully inside her purse and nervously fingered the sepia photograph of her sister. It had been taken when Hilda was twenty years old, now faded and indistinct. In her bag there was also a wallet. It contained five ten pound notes. She had saved and saved. Gradually over the years she put back the money she had 'borrowed', just as Hilda used to.

Clothilde did not doubt that she would find her sister, or someone who knew her. All she had to do was take the photo to a policeman, or to a Catholic church and ask. Of course she would have changed, she'd be older, but Clothilde did not think that she would be unrecognisable.

She had never been on such a long journey, and alone. She stared around the compartment, which was practically empty, and squeezed in behind a plastic table.

She felt her belly catch the edge. They don't give you much room, she thought. She would have to put her coat somewhere. Behind her a woman casually tossed hers up onto a ledge directly over the seat.

That's the way, she thought as she removed her heavy coat. The day was warm, but it was her best and she did not want to go all the way to London looking scruffy.

She stood up with difficulty, and making her coat into a bundle, aimed it at the ledge. It fell down again and wrapped itself about her shoulders. After four attempts she grew hot in the face and her arms ached.

'I'm sixty-eight,' she thought. 'God knows, I might be older.'

She looked around helplessly. The woman had settled behind a newspaper and a couple of young people further down had their backs towards her, and were wearing earphones. She could have danced a jig and no one would have been the wiser. She put her coat on her knees.

The train began to fill up. She smiled happily, waiting for someone to sit next to her so that she might start a conversation,

Those Sailing Ships of His Boyhood Dreams

but her eager eyes gave early warning to the other travellers.

Out of the window the industrial landscape slipped away, past Runcorn and the power plant chimneys, grey and massive, the disused machinery rusting where it had been left, the iron shifting devices for coal, and the coke containers, standing idle. The black buildings of the North, were washed and grey like weak impressions of their once great past, when they had been the industrial heart of the world.

The gleam of prosperity had not touched her as it glittered feebly over. The war took all the young men and left widows everywhere. She got married, just as Chamberlain promised them peace in our time. Her first husband only had one lung. In the street there were those who said he was pretending. It had not been easy. Other men had to go.

She was out in the munitions factory, the babies in the work crèche, and he was drinking away whatever money she earned. And it was good money. Strange that it needed a war to give her independence.

They heard about the heavy raid on London. It was autumn because they were roasting chestnuts in the street. The wireless said that whole areas had been flattened overnight. A man's voice described the hole in the roof of Saint Paul's looking straight up to God. They huddled around the wireless at her mother's. None of them said anything, but they all wondered if Hilda was alive.

What days, she thought. Then the soldiers returned. Local men walked about like strangers in suits which did not fit.

A neighbour's son had been in Trafalgar Square. He reckoned he'd seen Hilda in the crowd. The world went mad that day, everybody was out on the streets. That was the story they heard, that he had seen her with a soldier, a Yank he said, but wasn't everyone crazy then? No one slept that night, people talked to anyone, social barriers seemed to break down. Women asked men to dance and whistled after soldiers in the street. Land girls ran around in trousers, drove buses, wielded power torches, and learnt engineering. They wore make-up and jitterbugged. What days!

'Did he speak to her?' their mother asked. 'Did he find out where she lived?'

But all he'd managed was to nod and ask if she was all right, and she had grinned back and told him to say hello to everyone before the crowd pushed them apart. He had watched her until she went out of view.

'She looked wonderful,' he remarked. 'I'd a chap with me, we'd been stationed together, a little Glaswegian, red-haired, he used to keep us all laughing. He was all for tearing after her.'

'Has she re-married?' their mother asked. 'Does she know Frank got a divorce from her?'

'How could he tell that mother?' snapped Miriam. 'He only saw her in a crowd. She's alive, at least that's something.'

After the crèches shut, Clothilde had to manage on what her husband earned. It was rough for the kids. Then she was widowed. But she went on, enduring life, sometimes wondering if Hilda had thought it all through, because there were days when she would have run away if she could.

She sat back in her seat. For much of the journey she slept. She wondered how they got tea, because people were walking back with paper cups.

'Where did you get that from?' she asked a man, and he indicated that there was a buffet service further down, in the sixth or seventh carriage.

Clothilde nodded, terrified that if she went all that way she might never find her seat again, and her best coat would be well and truly lost. Just then a young student-looking woman leaned across and offered to bring her back something, as she was going to buy sandwiches. Clothilde gave her a pound coin.

'A cup of tea would be lovely' she smiled.

'Right, I'll sort out your change when I get back.'

Clothilde knew there would not be much and she laughed remembering how her first job paid four shillings and threepence a week. She could not begin to work that out in decimals, but she knew it was only a small coin nowadays.

She remembered the feel of the big pennies, satisfying if you got twelve together. Halfpennies and farthings weighed her purse down then. A silver shilling was something, and a half crown was only glimpsed on a Thursday night.

When the young woman returned, Clothilde, wanting to talk,

Those Sailing Ships of His Boyhood Dreams

asked her if she would like to see her sister, and fished the old photo out. The girl took it and studied it.

'I love the clothes,' she said as she handed it back. 'She was beautiful. When was that taken?'

Hilda was beautiful, that was a shock. She had never heard anyone else say so, but she had been fine-looking and they all knew it. No one ever referred to such things in her family. Hilda could twist people round her finger. People always wanted to believe her, because she looked so innocent.

And she knew that she had been taken in no less; for fifty years she had kept this image of her sister in her mind. That she had been led astray, that she had been witlessly taken in by someone. Hilda was not in control of circumstances. Clothilde had believed anything which made allowances for her sister.

'I'm going to meet her, I haven't seen her for fifty years,' she said.

The young woman seemed genuinely touched.

'Oh, that's grand,' she enthused. 'How nice for you! Heavens, it will be quite a reunion won't it?'

'It will be that all right,' Clothilde thought as she sipped her tea.

'Was she out in America or Australia, then?'

'Somewhere like that,' Clothilde smiled.

She wondered what her own children would make of their mother if they discovered she had gone off for a day in London? None of them were born when Hilda disappeared, but they had all heard her speak about her sister.

She wanted to return triumphant, telling them that she had found the lost member of their family, without causing too much fuss. If they discovered that she intended to come all this way on her own, they would worry and warn her. She was certain that some of them might insist on accompanying her, or worse still, try to dissuade her from setting out, try to tell her that it was a hopeless task.

Euston Station was enormous. Clothilde followed the ranks of people pouring out and up the platform. It opened out into a massive concourse where people rushed in all directions, or watched massive notice boards that flashed up destinations. It horrified her. She thought that she would never find her platform again. And she had imagined that she might find her sister.

She wondered what Hilda must have felt like stepping off that train, knowing that she would never go back. She had walked out into London, not knowing a soul, and wanting to make her way in the world. What had she done? Clothilde hoped that she had met the man from work. That it was an arrangement, because the thought of her sister alone and scared in some hotel made her shiver. Of course, she had all that money. Maybe she bought herself a place? But even a large sum of money would be used up over a few years. She hoped Hilda landed on her feet.

Clothilde could not cross the road, the traffic had to be seen to be believed, and the only thing that vaguely resembled a church had columns around it, with large women who held up the roof on their heads. Certainly not Catholic.

The constant noise of cars was exhausting. She wanted to get away from the sound, but she was scared if she turned up a smaller street, she might never find the station again.

Where was she going to start looking? She had no map of the city. What had she expected to find? A sympathetic priest? She sat down in some gardens. An old man in rags approached her and she gave him ten pence. An Indian family were playing with a ball. The woman threw it up in the air and a young man headed it, before one of the children caught it.

The woman wore a pink sari that blew in the wind, and her nose was pierced with a gold hoop. Her black hair reached to her waist, twisted in a thick plait. Clothilde liked families when they didn't argue.

She must have fallen asleep because when she looked up different people were walking round the gardens. A tall woman in a fur coat was walking a tiny dog with diamonds in its collar. This is London, they might be real.

Clothilde took a small brooch from her purse. It was a cat with green cut-glass eyes. She remembered the terrible row there had been, with Hilda accusing Agatha of taking it, while she, the youngest, sat, tight-lipped in the room.

She could never bring herself to own up after that. She hid the thing, hated it, but could never come clean. Agatha would have

Those Sailing Ships of His Boyhood Dreams

killed her for one thing, not only Hilda. She looked at it now, then put it carefully down on the bench. Someone else could come and find it. At least after fifty years she had tried to find Hilda, tried to give back what she had taken.

She settled onto the train comfortably this time, intending to take her shoes off and sleep. Out of habit she glanced inside her bag. She could not see the wallet! She pulled things out, her scarf, her comb, bus pass, keys, her small plastic purse, the faded photo, but no wallet. Five ten pound notes, such a lot of money. All in single notes once, so many, such an awful secret.

Suddenly, Clothilde started to laugh. Her eyes watered. She could not get her breath and her shoulders shook. A man next to her smiled.

'Someone must have told you a good one,' he said.

She nodded, unable to speak for laughing. She would have explained the joke to him, but she could not get the words out. He wouldn't have understood anyway. Very few people would know what she was talking about.

'I've been paid back,' she wheezed between guffaws. 'After fifty years! My sister Hilda, she hasn't changed. You could never leave anything down when she was around but she'd have it!'

The man nodded politely.

As the train pulled out of Euston, Clothilde took out her hankie, because she was no longer sure whether she was laughing or crying.

Burn Bright Those Yuletide Logs

Majella watched the twins pin socks to the back of the old armchair. They took safety pins and stuck them through the ankles and pushed them firmly up against the red stuff of the covers. She wondered at this, but they were a good year older and knew about things, both being at school already, so she followed suit.

School sounded a fine place to Majella. You sat in rows and a nice woman talked to you and read stories out of a book. But the bestest thing of all was something called Playtime when you went out into a big yard. There was so much space you could run round and round for ever without once knocking into anything.

You played games with other children. Once a man with a moustache who wore a shirt without any sleeves, ran round with them bouncing a ball. He had a whistle that hung from his neck on a piece of ribbon. And they had to line up and throw the ball to each other. Majella couldn't wait to go to school.

At home she was left alone in the day now that her mother was occupied with the new baby. It was cold in the house. Majella amused herself by twisting the draught excluders into shapes. Her mother made them out of old nylons and they lay like great serpents in front of all the doors.

Now it was dark before the twins came home. It was winter again they said knowledgeably, and they were excited because winter turned into Christmas. Majella could not remember Christmas but the twins explained that the ones before must have been missed. But they heard the other boys in their class talking. It seemed easy enough. All you had to do was remember to hang a sock up and in the morning it would be full of things. Only you had to do it on a special night, otherwise it just wouldn't work.

They shouted each other down in their eagerness to tell their mother.

'They get filled with toys, nuts ... '

'Sweets ... ' the other shouted.

'Silver sixpences and oranges ... ' They nodded their heads, breathlessly. 'Can we have a tree with lights, like the ones we saw in the windows last time, can we?'

'Go on, please. If you have a tree there might be even bigger things in the morning, only you must have a tree for those ... '

The tallest twin watched his mother's blank face.

'We can just hang socks up can't we? We've got socks.'

Mrs Ryan looked wearily at her children. The baby was crying in the pram as it had been all morning. Her head throbbed with the sound. The twins' bright faces were more than she could bear. Yet something in her resisted telling them the truth. Then she shrugged. What was the point? They could not afford childhood.

But even after there was no Father Christmas, their spirits could not be diminished. To have lost someone so recently acquired made it hard for the figure to be missed. He was too sudden a novelty for the twins to feel that they ever possessed him. But Mrs Ryan was a responsible woman. She warned the pair about telling others at school what they had learned. Just because childhood was too expensive for them, it didn't mean everyone else had to go without.

She trusted the twins. Like two tiny men already, they worried about their mother's health. They stood in front of her when their father was in a bad mood. But that sullen Majella had her beaten. As long as the girl kept from under her feet, they could get by.

Majella crept and was silent. She knew not to ask questions and had once felt her mother's hard hand for laughing too loudly.

'You think life's all a joke, you little idiot, don't you? Well you'll learn the hard way. It's not all play!' and she struck the girl across the face until Majella no longer laughed.

To laugh meant you were gone soft. They did not see their mother smile much. Once Majella asked the twins and they told her that only dopes and lunatics went round with grins on their faces. It was easier to cry. Majella discovered that if you cried you were left alone. Not that there was anywhere to go at home. There were only two rooms which weren't damp. Sometimes she would hear her mother screaming at her father. Those days she always managed to get hit, no matter what she did. She would hide

Burn Bright Those Yuletide Logs

behind a door until it was over, or cower in the cupboard under the stairs.

Mrs Ryan wondered what the good of a daughter was. The girl irritated her. But ever since her husband started his builder's yard, everything irritated her. Their own house fell down around them and he was too damned busy with other people's homes to fix theirs.

'Another man would have this sorted out. Would have made this into a decent home for his family. But not you. No. What the hell have you ever done? And how long have we been here? Six years and we're still in the same two rooms.'

She placed her hand over her belly which was beginning to show signs of increase.

'I hope you're not bloody pregnant again,' he said.

'Damn you!' she screamed. 'You think it's nothing to do with you. You carry on like Jack the Lad while you've no time for the kids you've got. And they came home today wondering why they've missed out on Christmas. Don't think you can fob them off, they're not babies any more. They won't be so easily fooled this time.'

Then he got pious and told her that the mass they went to on Christmas morning was more important than any stories of men coming through the roof. He wanted to know when he had denied them anything for their souls. Didn't he always take them to see the crib in church, he said. And that was far better than letting them grow up like other kids who didn't even know what they were celebrating.

But she was having none of it.

'You tight-fisted bastard,' she spat. Religion was free, and it was all they could afford to give them.

'I hate your miserable God if he's too mean to let my kids have Christmas like all the others. I'll not go inside that stinking church. Get the lousy priest down here. I'll show him how we live. I'll take him round and show him the place. We're cramped into two rooms because of you and your business. While you're out doing building work for others your own family has to live like animals.'

That made him nervous. She knew that he had to keep in with the priest if he was to get the contract for the church roof.

Those Sailing Ships of His Boyhood Dreams

'You don't know how a business works,' he yelled at her and she called him a fool if he thought he did.

But she knew nothing of mortgages, ownership or any of the words the sharp young man in the suit had used when he first took them round the house. She only remembered the terrible smell of damp. In one room she could see the sky through the roof. But he reassured her that it would be all right. He would see to it.

'We're getting it cheap because of all the work that needs doing. After all, aren't I a builder? I know what I'm about.'

'Well, you're certainly in the necessary profession for a place like this,' the young man told him and he beamed at the word 'profession'. That was what he had, a calling, not a mere job.

He always wanted his own business, his own home, because as a boy his family had owned nothing. They said he would go far because he was the one with ambition. Even as a boy he'd wanted to have his own bike and he'd worked weekends until he could pay for a racer on the weekly.

She did not know if she had ever loved him. Love was a stupid word, but he seemed to have an energy about him that the others lacked. With him she thought she might do well. He had the air of a businessman then.

'My husband's in business,' she would be able to say to the girls behind the counter where she once worked.

But it was always the business. The business this, the business that. She was worn out hearing it.

At the start she thought she might help. She could do the paperwork. They would be a partnership. But he told her that he was more efficient.

'You don't know anything about business. You've no idea how deals are struck.'

The way he earned their living was not to be her concern. Then he went on and bought the house, even as she told him she didn't like it. He reminded her that he paid the bills and therefore he made the decisions. She did not even have a vote in their lives. And she could smell the damp creeping up on them.

Upstairs they used one room and kept the doors to the others tightly sealed so the smell would not permeate everywhere.

'I'll get those floor boards replaced,' he told her shortly after they moved in, when she first saw the rotting timber close up. But

Burn Bright Those Yuletide Logs

they had been there six years and the same planks were on those floors. She imagined she could see them getting worse. A dank tidal wave of seeping wetness left traces on the landing. She saw wet stains as the secret midnight bather left tracks along the floor.

After the first year the parlour became unlivable in and they retreated to the kitchen. Crowded into two rooms in the weeping house she had dreams. Fish swam past her in the night. Once she saw a man with an aqualung who appeared like a windowcleaner to scrape the barnacles from the panes of glass. She was on the *Lusitania*, sunk years before. She picked up broken glass in the ruined ballroom where only the seaweed danced.

'A good fire in the grate would dry out most of it,' he told her.

The wallpaper she put up in anticipation that first year, was spongy with wet patches, like great blisters under its surface.

They could not use the parlour as a room to sit in so he started to fill it up with bricks and planks of wood from the warehouse. But even these were not destined for them. They were intended for work he was doing on another house. Never the one he lived in. She had to climb across his stuff to change the curtains for she was determined that outside on the street, the house should at least look respectable.

When he hired the work-yard he began to spend much of his time in it. He did not feel how cramped they had become at home, or see that the kids were growing. He was seldom there. Instead, of an evening he stretched out with his mates in a pub. He came home late most nights and crawled over the beds which were laid end to end, to get at his wife.

She had lost all interest. It meant more kids for her. The twins were all right, but she had no heart for Majella nor the baby. And now she felt sick in the morning again. If there was something she could take to get rid of it she would.

She'd had a daughter the first time, a beautiful child. How she'd loved that one. God in his wisdom had taken her from them. Now her husband never mentioned the child's name. As if she'd never existed. Rose, a little tiny thorn she'd been. But she wouldn't let herself cry. What was the use of daughters? They break your heart.

When the twins were born he'd cried. It was the only time she'd seen him do that.

'They'll be strong,' he said. 'They'll grow into men. Ryan and Sons we'll be. You wait.'

Then Majella arrived. Like her father she was dark and silent. A mysterious child that Mrs Ryan couldn't warm to.

On Christmas Eve she told them that they were not hanging socks up in the bedroom. 'I don't want you crawling all over me and the baby at some awful hour,' she told them. 'Take them downstairs'.

In the morning, no doubt Baby Jesus was being lain out in the manger up in the church. At the same time, three ecstatic children took their socks from the armchair back. In the bedroom even Mrs Ryan was smiling.

She heard their squeals of delight as they pulled out the cheap plastic toys she had got at the market that week. She put on the old coat that hung behind the door and shuffled downstairs in time to see them pulling out loose sweets, and witness the marvel of an apple and an orange each. Their eyes shone with the scene of such plenty and she remembered another Christmas long ago when she had won the doll at a party held for the family of seamen.

It was a big doll with two flaxen plaits and a chalk face that always grinned even after an ugly crack disfigured it. That had been the present to end all presents when she was a child. There had been times after that when she had received gifts from the charity foundation, but she never wanted more, she could say that honestly. Not after that doll. But then no one made the fuss they do now about Christmas. After the war it became such a big event. An awful, expensive time to survive. Now her children had discovered it, she would approach each successive one with dread.

'Mum! Mum!' the children shouted when they saw her at the door.

'It's true, it's true! The socks really do get filled up!'

They were jumping around. Majella had wet herself.

'Is that right?' she asked feigning amazement. 'Me and your father should have hung one up in that case.'

Quietly Majella came up behind her mother. Silent, hoping she wouldn't notice her accident. Her lip trembled as she held out her hand.

'What the hell do you want now?' The words were out before she could stop them. She saw the small orange offered on her daughter's upturned palm. The girl's eyes irritated her. It was as if she was always on the verge of tears. She pushed the child away from her. The orange rolled to the ground. Upstairs she heard the baby crying and went to it.

But it was to be a day of surprises. He had come to bed late. He was sweating. What he'd been up to she couldn't guess. She turned her back to him and went to sleep.

'I've something for all of you, for Christmas,' he announced later that morning.

In the parlour they climbed over stacks of wood and dodged the piles of corrugated iron he was storing.

'Isn't the work-yard big enough for you,' she said, 'that now you have to start bringing it all home?'

First the damp forced them out. Now other things invaded. Their home was being taken over by a giant hermit crab. She thought she could see rust on the metal ladders propped against the wall.

'You'll ruin them leaving them there. The damp destroys everything.'

She thought how hopeless it was, the rooms were useless even as storage space.

'There's nothing a good warm fire in the grate won't dry out,' he always said.

They struggled across the obstacle course. Then she saw it. A tree. He'd gone out and bought one for the kids. It was enormous. It stood in a pot he'd decorated with bits of silver foil and tinsel.

He crossed over to the side and turned on a switch. Instantly, dozens of tiny, coloured lights appeared. He'd been careful to place it well inside the window so that it could be seen in the street.

They shivered in the cold room. The lights gave no heat. Then they climbed back out and left it, fairy bulbs shining on the corrugated metal sheets stacked against the walls.

The only way to look at their tree was to stand out in the street and watch through the window like passers-by. But the kids were proud. They had a tree like everyone else. People would stop and look at it and imagine the cosy scene surrounding it.

She wanted to spit. Her silence made him wild. Her stony expression was hateful. Later they heard the front door slam.

Majella could not understand what was happening. It had been a day of wonder. And the following day there was silence in the house. Neither parent talked much. That afternoon her father went out again.

'If you come home drunk I'm locking that front door,' her mother screamed after him.

Out on the street a stranger answered sardonically, 'and a merry Christmas to you love.'

Then their mother was inside giving instructions.

'Quickly. Put on your coats.'

'Where are we going?' the twins wanted to know, but Majella said nothing. She understood that it was to be another mystery.

'Come on. We might just go to the park. You can have a run round.'

It was a mild Christmas that year and there was no snow, but she made them wrap up warmly.

'It might get chilly later on,' she said. She was in such a hurry that she wouldn't wait for them to button everything up.

'You can do that on the street,' she snapped at the tallest twin. Then at the front door she suddenly darted back as if she had forgotten something.

'Wait there.'

She went into the parlour. They heard her climbing over the piles of wood and iron. When she reappeared she shut the door carefully behind her.

'Come on, come on,' she flapped. 'Don't stand about,' and they were on the street and being hurried along

On the corner Majella turned back to have a look at their tree. She was so proud. It shimmered in the window. All the tiny lights were on. Her eyes danced, and the tree looked like the candled altar in the church when they lit up hundreds for Quarant'Ore when, if she stared hard enough, the flames would merge together. The altar seemed to swim in front of her eyes as the candle points flickered and leapt.

'Hurry up, stop gawping!' her mother shouted. She pushed the girl in front of her.

A fire. A good fire to get rid of the damp. Their mother did not look back at the tree as they turned the corner. She didn't need to, she knew by then it would be blazing.

A Fine Voice You Have Ma'am

Your mother was dead before I ever heard her sing. As a child I must have heard her round your house whenever I went over, but now I can't remember if she had any sort of a singing voice at all, or if it was just average. I suppose that in those narrow corridors and low ceilinged rooms, an ordinary voice would swell and fill the space, and to those who listened it might have sounded rather grand.

Before she was married she had won a talent contest at Butlins. She was working the season and staff weren't normally supposed to enter, but someone dropped out at the last minute so they let her step in.

'Don't let on you work here,' the supervisor warned. 'I know no one out there will recognise you, it's not as if you're on the entertainment side of things, but kitchen staff are still employees and it says here that employees and members of their family are not normally eligible. They have to put that in, otherwise you'd have people saying it was all fixed.'

Anyhow, she won it. She could remember their faces the next morning out by the big aluminium sink.

'They didn't know I could sing. They were shocked. All the next day they kept coming up to me, they were that surprised. "We had no idea" they said,' and she would flush with pride, retelling the old story.

But she must have wondered then why there was no recording contract, no talent scout (and that was the place for them in those days, she always said), nobody to pick her out, to give her a slot in an end-of-pier review.

So she finished the summer season and travelled home on the charabanc. The pink rosette was crushed in her luggage and when she pinned it up on her bedroom wall at home the number and legend 'First' had faded.

But one cold November night after her triumph she was called back for an encore by the manager of the pub where she had stood up on singers' night. A man buying a round of drinks sent one over. She blushed and he grinned at her across the room. When she finished her encore he came over. He would have made a pass you see, she told them, but he didn't because she was somebody.

'When you've a gift, a talent, call it what you will, you are different. People know. They can tell. You stand apart from the crowd. He could tell, that man. He saw what was in me and was respectful. He waited with me and asked if he could order me a taxi. He wasn't like those loud ones my mother was always warning me about.'

She never saw him again, but always remembered the way he looked at her as she put the microphone back on its rest. He followed her with his eyes as she came down from the raised platform in the lounge bar.

She would have sung another, but it was last orders and the pianist was slow.

She dreamed of a career. A lucky break was all she needed. She had wanted to get noticed. Others did. It must have annoyed her to think of it. Even Rosemary Clooney must have started somewhere. And that Ruby Murray. What did you make of her? she'd say. The cut of her. And already on the front of magazines wearing a red sequinned dress like a great hussy.

Her mother said that pubs and such weren't places for nice girls. And they weren't. She couldn't go in unescorted, and after her mate got married and stopped going out nights, there was little else she could do. She sat in. Then she married a local lad herself. And not a drinker either. Her mother approved.

Sometimes when the kids were all at home, she would sing tracks from musicals. She took them to see *Carousel*, *Oklahoma* and *The King and I* and would sing the tunes all week long, making up the words when she couldn't remember.

Once, she dished the tea up singing 'Getting to Know You'. She went round the table singing the lines:

'Getting to know you, getting to know all about you. Getting to like you, getting to hope you like me ...' And she stopped at their shoulders to stare into each of their faces in turn. She smiled with

A Fine Voice You Have Ma'am

a strange, hard smile, pulling her face as she remembered Deborah Kerr doing for the King of Siam's children.

She seemed disappointed that they did not suddenly sprout top knots, while you told me years later that you had been upset because your mother wasn't as slim as the movie star. But the children became embarrassed while their mother grimaced and sang in proper English, careful to sound the ending of every word. She glanced repeatedly to the window where the curtains were still not shut, as if she was waiting for something to happen, for lights to go on and a film crew to appear.

Once in the park she sang and a family, picnicking nearby, stopped talking to listen. Encouraged by the attention her voice rose, louder and bolder. She would entertain the entire playing-field given half a chance.

Her dreams were slipping away. Now younger singers appeared on the covers of the *Record Mirror*. And she was a married woman, she told everyone. Married women don't go on stage. Not with kids to look after.

'I lost my chance,' she told her children.

She was dead before they dug out the cassette tapes. Alone and widowed she sat in recording her voice on the machine her son bought her so that she could send talking letters to him and his wife in Australia.

'This is one of my mam's: some traditional stuff,' you said, slipping it in.

We waited as the tape whirred into place. Then an old woman's voice came out. It was ear-shatteringly high, and the singer was breathless. The voice was wavery and flat in places. It kept missing notes and because it was unaccompanied, we heard all the breathy pauses the instrumentalist of her imagination filled.

I wondered if she ever played it back to herself. If she ever heard the fine voice of her memory reduced to this shrill sound.

You stopped the tape suddenly and shook your head.

'God, but I can't listen to that,' you said. 'It's worse than I remember.'

Deceitful, peaceful silence won us.

'Did she have a good voice, then?' I asked.

'Who knows,' you said, not wanting to take away the last hope that died with her.

A Well Travelled Woman

My Aunt Mairead's most cherished possession was kept inside a little buff carton printed with the words 'Stereoscope Pour Positifs'. It was a black hollow box-shaped piece of equipment with two peepholes at one end and a piece of clear film at the other.

When you put the special slides in the back and looked through the lens your sight went funny for a bit because the slides, which were all black and white shots of Lourdes, were made up of two identical photographs, and your eyes would dance between one and the other. But if you held the stereoscope still for a few seconds, the picture settled. As it merged into one image, a wonderful thing happened. People began to stand out.

There were three dimensions in that funny little viewer. The pictures became rounded until Lourdes was no longer a flat memory but a real world. If you put a hand out you would touch the faces of those attending benediction.

I half expected someone to move and duck behind a column in the photograph taken outside the Church of the Rosary. There were pictures of people who queued, eternally patient, to fill bottles with water from taps in the grotto. In one an old woman leans her elbow on a wall and her head is turned to speak to another behind her. I always wondered what she said. Did she know her photograph had been taken?

Great leather wheelchairs rested in the sun and the Red Cross wore funny hats like nuns. That was the Lourdes of my Aunt Mairead where she had been moved deeply by everything she saw.

'You can't beat the torchlight procession,' she'd say, staring into space. 'The Lady Day March in May's not a patch on it. Can you imagine it now? It stretches back for miles. Hundreds of souls each carrying a flickering candle, each praying for a miracle and

Those Sailing Ships of His Boyhood Dreams

not a Protestant in sight.'

Aunt Mairead was the most exotic person I knew. She had crossed the channel and seen another world. It took her two years to save up the money, paying every week into the Pilgrimage Fund when Ron McCarthy came round with his little red ledger on a Thursday evening. But she was determined. Ever since she was a girl she longed to travel abroad and she dreamed about visiting Lourdes, the most famous of all shrines to the Virgin.

She was genuinely religious. It was a good thing because her faith must have been sorely tested by the rigours of the journey. Her friends had seen her off an able-bodied person, but by all accounts she was so ill at the other end that she had to be taken from the train on a stretcher by the Red Cross. She must have been shocked by the length of the journey for nothing could have prepared her for that. Any sea journey was torture to Mairead at the best of times, but to find that she had to board yet another train for the longest part of the route after surviving the boat must have been as much as she could endure. The cramped conditions and the heat in carriage class caused her to faint repeatedly. On arrival her appearance must have been terrible because the brancardiers, who were waiting for an invalid train on the next platform and were used to transporting the sick and dying to and from the grotto, suggested that she be taken to a hospice instead of the hotel. She remained for three days in a paupers' ward, because the parish had only taken out minimum insurance.

Later, she said that she was too dispirited to care, but as her malaise subsided she began to feel frustrated. This was Lourdes the Wonderful and she was missing it. She managed to persuade a kind-hearted nun to push her out to the grotto, where she was left all afternoon like an overgrown baby in the sun.

The sight of all the serious invalids made her feel cowardly and she determined to rejoin her group now that her strength had returned. She was bothered about her suitcase which she had been separated from. Before they left, Father O'Flynn had said they might find some of the customs quite different and had warned them to keep an eye on their handbags. She had a good lace mantilla in her case among other things and was anxious to check that her black strap shoes were still where she'd packed them. This accomplished she insisted on going with the pilgrim group to the evening service so that she could give thanks.

She had seen enough of the inside of strange corridors and rooms to last her a lifetime. She had scrimped and saved just to be there and she wanted to be out in it, seeing, hearing, and grateful for the faculties in a place full of those who could do neither. She wanted to move around freely. All she had managed since her arrival was sitting among the dying for an afternoon, unable to get her wheelchair to reverse.

Martha Kilhooley, who carried the pennant for the Legion of Mary in the May procession, was impressed by my aunt's determination to attend the service.

'You couldn't have kept her back,' she used to say in years to come. 'Just up from her sick bed, and wouldn't stay in the hotel, but she'd have to be out at mass giving thanks to Our Blessed Mother.'

On Saturday afternoons they would take tea together and swop memories. Martha had been to Lourdes eight times and was known as The Continental because she was always telling the neighbours there was nothing like travel to give a person an education.

'Indeed the young women now isn't like that. All they're concerned about is having a good time. I remember telling Mairead, Now only if you're up to it, I said. God knows how you've suffered just to be here. There's no sin in you staying comfortable in the hotel room. You can pray just as well from there, I said, but she'd have none of it.'

Neither Martha nor my aunt ever married. Their ideal man was a cross between someone with the selflessness of a missionary priest and Saint Francis of Assisi, because he was kind to animals. There can't have been many round our way who measured up.

But on Saturday afternoons over tea and shop-bought cakes in Martha Kilhooley's parlour they let the stereoscope transport them into another world. It was a strange one where much of the population was sick or dying, but where there was always an abundance of willing helpers. Where there were more nuns and priests per square foot than any other place in the world. And the language was softly spoken.

'Entry, that's a French word,' Aunt Mairead told me. 'And

when they give you something you say Mercy, as if they might be going to kill you.' She giggled at the illogicality of foreigners.

'When you've travelled like me,' The Continental said, 'you get to know how to treat them. Sure, they're no different from us, there are good foreigners, like there are bad ones of your own.'

'San Ferry Ann,' the breadman told me. 'That's French.'

'French letters,' his delivery boy said and was given a clip round the ear. But The Continental had learned to speak it, she could say the entire Hail Mary.

'Oh go on Martha,' Mairead would entreat her. 'It makes it seem so . . . oh I don't know, foreign.' And brushing away the last crumbs from her second slice of almond gâteau The Continental would clear her throat and begin.

'Je Vous salue Marie, pleine de grace.' Her voice would sweep and fall theatrically.

They held fast to the miracle of Lourdes, even when some who had been on pilgrimage began to doubt openly that it had ever worked.

'Remember Jack Traynor!' they were fond of telling those of little faith. But those who doubted said there were often other reasons for cures. And weren't some of those illnesses odd anyway? Who knows if someone's really blind or not, the sceptics said.

But Jack Traynor had been crippled and he walked down the platform at Lime Street Station.

Explain that.

The Continental had a pamphlet from the Catholic Truth Society. She'd wave it in their faces if they dared to challenge her.

'Look at this,' she said. '*I Met a Miracle: The Story of Jack Traynor*. Eleven and three halfpence. They can get their own copies. They make me sick, these knowalls.'

It was in the papers, years ago. The *Liverpool Post* gave it headline space. LOURDES PILGRIMS RETURN. PARALYSED MAN ABLE TO WALK.

The reporters had been waiting. The man had sent a telegram to his wife. 'Am better', it said.

EXTRAORDINARY SCENES WERE WITNESSED AT LIME STREET STATION ON SATURDAY NIGHT WHEN 400 PILGRIMS, FORMING PART

OF THE GREAT LANCASHIRE CONTINGENT WHO LEFT FOR LOURDES EIGHT DAYS AGO, ARRIVED BACK.

'I WAS UP BY SAINT GEORGE'S WHEN I SAW CROWDS OF PEOPLE, AND POLICEMEN WITH BATONS PUSHING THEM,' A BYSTANDER SAYS.

Mairead could rattle off the press stories that accompanied the event, even though the man himself was dead before she went on her pilgrimage.

For some reason his miracle was never accredited, the medical report was never received by the diocese. But Jack Traynor was their hero, as Saint Bernadette was their saint.

'He's living proof of God's mercy,' Mairead said.

'I thought he died years ago,' my father said.

'He was living proof while he was alive,' my mother shouted, 'which is more than you are.'

But miracles or not, Mairead fell in love with Lourdes. When she spoke about it I could smell the candles burning in the grotto, feel the cool evening air as she felt it on her stroll back to the hotel.

She remembered the narrow streets crowded with establishments with religious sounding names: The Golgotha, The Vatican, The Angelus, Our Lady of the Sorrows, even The Hotel of the Immaculate Conception, which she would not have liked to stay in, just to be on the safe side. And the hundreds of souvenir shops selling medals and cheap tin and plaster statues of the Virgin. There must have been hundreds of strings of rosary beads which shopkeepers hung over sticks to catch the sun like so many brightly coloured baubles, as the traders vied with each other for business in prayer cards and wax candles.

'Every day I lit a candle in the grotto. The heat from thousands of them was incredible. And my small prayer was there among them.'

That was the only time in her life that she had owned a bathing suit, which she bought specially thinking she would need one to take the waters in the holy spring. Bathing in Lourdes was something she knew she must do, it was an essential part of the pilgrimage.

Mairead was terrified of water. She would not even take her shoes off at the seaside. But it was more like taking a bath, than a swim, the experienced pilgrims told her. Her party had all been while she was ill, but Father O'Flynn fixed it so that she could join another group. There were always steady queues of people waiting to get into the baths. Mairead couldn't bring herself to look at them, and told Father O'Flynn that if she was causing too much trouble she didn't mind missing, because she could always wash her feet under the taps outside the shrine, and she would be just as satisfied with that.

'The bath is essential to the Lourdes experience, my child. It wouldn't be fair for you to come all this way and miss it,' and he smiled kindly at her generosity of spirit.

It was not as public as she feared. There was a changing room with cubicles and she left her clothes on a peg. They made her leave her bathing suit there as well and volunteers handed her a plain cotton shift, which was still wet from the previous bather. Getting into that was the most difficult part and she felt so peculiar that she was glad to be among strangers.

The volunteers pointed her towards three stone steps which led into the grey bath. The water was completely still and she could not see the bottom, or guess how deep it might be. She had been told that they frowned on total immersion because it held up the proceedings, so trusting it would not cover her head, she stepped out into freezing water. It came up to her hips and before she knew where she was, she was struggling to walk through it with the borrowed robe billowing around her. The volunteers shouted something which she didn't understand. They indicated that she ought to sit or kneel and one raced out on the bit of duckboard by the side and pushed her shoulder down. Water took her breath away as it covered her chest. And then she could not say what happened, she must have slipped, because a film of ice seemed to cover her face. It numbed her cheeks. Her one great fear was of drowning. She had never put her ears under water in her life and now she was hearing those odd water sounds as everything was swallowed by the liquid which was swallowing her.

Rouoo, rouoo, rouoo, deep-voiced water said. The green sentences were stretched thinly until they broke into single letters, which sucked water like drinking straws through their hollow-tubed legs. Full up, they became swollen and deadly white like tubercular milk bottles on the doorstep at home. But home was a long way away and the letters regrouped into senseless foreign words. Rouoo, rouoo, rouoo.

Water trickled through her ears into her head. She felt it fill up her mind and seep through her skin turning her veins to water, and she was floating in the rouoo, rouoo, rouoo, drowning in its forgetful, faithless embrace. She must breathe, she must reach the surface.

Water broke around her. A volunteer pulled her upright and she gasped and shuddered. She must have had her head under for barely seconds, but the watery clock ticking in the belly of the holy spring said otherwise. It had moved its heavy, waterlogged fingers and its sonorous ticking said rouoo, rouoo, rouoo.

The timepiece pulsed its hours through the green ripples and she coughed, afraid that she would make a fool of herself. The volunteer rushed her out of the public bath and held up a tiny picture of Our Lady of Lourdes for her to kiss. She had done it. For ever after she would recommend Lourdes as opposed to any other holy water. She kept a bottle on top of the piano and would bless herself regularly with the substance of her triumph over evil. For she knew now what lurked under calm lakes. Her particular devil was green and wet, a shell-covered, misshapen thing that wrecked ships and counted time backwards. That afternoon was to remain with her all her life.

'You mustn't dry yourself after. You just have to get dressed as best you can.'

She remembered that everything stuck to her. Her stockings twisted and creased round her ankles. Elastic snapped back away from her. She had put her slip on and without thinking started to rub it round over her front, before she realised. 'You just have to let the water dry on you.'

'It's torture entirely,' Martha Killhooley agreed, 'the miracle is we don't all come back with pneumonia.' And they would both laugh. But Mairead said that for the rest of the day her body did tingle, and she had a wonderful sense of relief. But after that she could never imagine why anybody should go swimming by way of recreation.

She had a lovely glittering rosary of red glass beads which turned greeny-blue in the light. On the central medal before the crucifix, was a scene depicting Bernadette when she first saw Aquero, as the peasant's daughter referred to the Lady in their local dialect.

On the reverse side was a glass window with the words 'Eau de Lourdes' punched in the metal surround and a clear liquid sealed inside.

'Just think, she was only fourteen when she saw Her first. She could hardly write her name.'

'Lots of saints were stupid,' my father said. 'God sometimes chooses fools to do his business because they're without sin.'

'We could do with less cleverness round here, and a bit more goodness,' my mother would snap back. 'The simple faith of children was good enough for Christ and it's good enough for me.'

Aunt Mairead's faith may have been simple but she was none the less a realist. She returned home knowing that it was one thing to be Bernadette Soubirous in the nineteenth century, and live in picturesque poverty with a father that hauled dirty linen for a hospital, but it was quite another to be unemployed in Liverpool with a father who delivered coal on the back of a wagon. She knew what romance was. It illuminated a drab life – like the brightly coloured beads of so many rosaries taken up by the faithful on feastdays to Our Lady.

Sometimes on Saturday afternoons she and The Continental would sing 'Bring flowers of the fairest', and could not prevent themselves from weeping, especially at the words, 'Lilies of the valley', for they were Mary's special flowers. They were the flowers she carried when she first appeared to Bernadette. I had a head-dress made out of plastic ones, only they had begun to yellow like the net veil I wore on Lady Day when the junior school walked in procession. But these sung lilies were beautiful, defied description and made grown women cry.

Then I would long to live in Lourdes, and go to the torchlight procession every night. I could get a room in a pension, and live just by the grotto. I would earn my living teaching English.

'That's your sister's fault. She's been filling her head up with daft ideas again,' my father said.

But it was a wonderful vision, of escape and otherworldliness. And there was no laughter like Aunt Mairead's. No one ever matched her, for happiness which was infectious or for sorrow which left you desolate.

She and Martha would cry over newspaper stories. Their

favourite was the one about Sparkle the little black and white mongrel who got run over. There was a photograph of the owner looking sadly at the camera while holding the dead body of Sparkle who looked as if he was sleeping. The owner must have considered the newsworthy potential of his pet even as it breathed its last. But Aunt Mairead trusted in the man's decency. She cut the story out and kept it folded between the pages of a book.

'Look at the little dog, looking at him as if to say "Why did you tell me it was safe to cross when it wasn't. Why did you say it was all right?"'

IT WILL BE ON MY CONSCIENCE FOR EVER, GRIEF STRICKEN OWNER SAYS.

'Wouldn't you feel awful if it was you?' Martha Kilhooley used to say, and they would sit over their tea feeling awful.

The obedience of the dog was what touched them most.

'Such a trusting little thing.'

'Poor Sparkle.'

'You have to trust God,' Aunt Mairead said. 'They wanted Bernadette put away in an asylum for incurables, but she kept on. She wouldn't take back what she'd seen.'

'Would you, Mairead?' The Continental asked her.

'Oh, I don't know. I've never had a vision.'

'I wonder what it's like, you know, seeing someone?' And they would imagine themselves, holding out against the ignorance of others. Alone in our street full of infidels and the ungodly, my Aunt Mairead and The Continental lit candles in their stark bedrooms. And watched each other growing old.

They counted themselves lucky, they had seen the sick and the dying lined up on leather stretchers for the last hope of the hopeless, waiting patiently at the hospital of faith for a cure defying medical science.

Mairead had been shocked by the sight of so much flesh exposed to the air, bandages removed, ready for the priest's touch, for another blessing, for the holy waters, for the intercession of the faithful, for prayers, hymns, for all the despair of the suffering in this world, and for Aquero's offer, 'I don't promise to make you happy in this world, but in the next.'

Lourdes displayed the most barbarous acts of nature and she agonised at the workings of her God and prayed. Here they were granted a respite from despair, if only for as long as the holy waters took to chill leaving them sodden and chastened. A minute of hope in a lifetime of abandon. And the promise of the next, not this world, but the next. And she understood and lit her yellow candles.

She wanted me to have the stereoscope when she died. Her shaking hands had scrawled my name on the buff carton, just to be on the safe side. She'd been adamant that the simple amusement, the 'child's toy' as my father called it, be left with someone who valued it and in my early enthusiasm I had shown myself to be a worthy custodian.

It came, packed carefully between two eggboxes with different coloured scraps of tissue paper that she'd saved. It was secured by an elastic armband of the type men once wore to keep their shirt cuffs straight, a respectable item that was no longer fashionable and circled the two halves of the eggbox like a mourner's dark ribbon. This was her greatest treasure.

As I looked through the slides, I found faces I remembered. The images of Lourdes were exactly as I'd seen them years ago. Inside the box, time had been arrested. I recognised the same people in the close-up shots, the procession, the blessing of the sick. It was familiar. But for the first time, I noticed how silent it had become now that Mairead was no longer there to fill up the background with noises, arguing and discussing with her friend about what they remembered. Now, with her dead, nobody spoke, there was no chant of prayers outside the basilica at the open air service, no gush of excitement at the appearance of a bishop, and the hollow baths were still.

A piece of paper fell out of the box. It was a handbill advertising the funicular railway. I opened it out.

DON'T LEAVE LOURDES AND THE PYRENEES, it warned in large blue letters, WITHOUT ASCENDING THE PIC DU JER. It promised an unrivalled view over the French and Spanish Pyrenees. WHEN BOOKING, INSIST UPON FUNICULAIRE DU PIC DU JER. SEE THE BASILICA AND SANCTUARIES. MAGNIFICENT PROSPECT OVER LOURDES.

And for a moment the silence broke. Mairead would have been shrieking with excitement. She was scared of heights. The old wooden train must have shook and thumped as it crawled upwards. And when she looked out, Lourdes would be shrinking.

Below, thousands of humans scuttled round in meaningless patterns. For Mairead there was still an all-loving God. That was comforting to think. Someone who could pick out individuals, could recognise a single soul in the heaving mass of humanity, and know them precisely, down to the last groove and swirl of their thumbprint.

Down below, she had seen dark shapes converging into solid wedges – a narrow strip wending its way along the river possibly. The world that day must have felt blue-peaked and enormous.

The train rattled and banged. Lourdes grew smaller. The pain congregating in clusters, faded. The sky opened and the air was clear and sweet, rising over the presence of suffering. Higher, higher, and beyond to where there was perfection and purity. The place where every prayer ascended, every mouthing of belief since the dawn of thought, every word rose here and swelled the sky, reaching a deafening plateau of noise and brilliance, which climbed still further up, up and beyond, until it joined the vastness of Mairead's faith.

*Those Sailing Ships
of His Boyhood Dreams*

My father was one for surprises. Suddenly, out of nowhere, the fait accompli was pulled like a rabbit and he'd stand there with the soft look of someone who knew they'd failed, but still grinned desperately in the hope of convincing us otherwise. It was an idiot's grin like the laughing death's head my friend's father wore on his arm. Death Before Dishonour his skin read and the tattooed teeth grimaced. He always wore long sleeves, even on the hottest days, and said he'd been a fool when he was young.

My friend showed me snap-shots of him leaning against a motor bike.

'Don't you think he looked like James Dean? It's odd to think he's me dad and now he works for the Co-op.'

When he met your mam he wore a leather jacket.

My own father wasn't so exciting. Not even with the knack he had of turning everything into a surprise. His surprises felt like a series of shocks that I could have lived without. Like the time I came home from school to discover he'd knocked through the bedroom doors and inserted panels of bubble glass where the wood used to be.

That night the landing light played off and on.

'How the hell can I see where I'm going in the dark – I'll break my neck on those stairs.'

'And how do you expect me to sleep if there's a light on outside the door?'

From the front bedroom my father thundered, 'Will ye get back to bed. You're waking the soddin' house up!'

Behind their panel we could see our mother moving around, her head out of shape and swollen. When she peered close to the glass she had six eyes. 'What's going on?' she said.

His back disappeared into the room. We watched the dancing red stripes of his pyjamas. He rippled.

Those Sailing Ships of His Boyhood Dreams

'Creatures of habit,' I heard him say. 'They won't put up with anything new.'

Light has always disturbed me. The thinnest crack under a door is sufficient to wake me, while my oldest brother was the opposite. He claimed to not be able to sleep if it was completely dark and always kept a light by his bed.

'Put out your light – it's shining through me door.'

And then my father would turn nasty with the complaints.

'What do you mean it's like being spied on? It'll stop you getting up to anything peculiar. Jesus, they'll be asking for locks on their doors next!'

And my mother would get out the Holy Water and sprinkle the site of the argument to bless away anger. Any carpets in our house were always soaking.

For years after the introduction of bubble glass, I never slept an unbroken night at home. I suppose I adapted the way a camel does for the desert. I became an insomniac. It stood me in good stead for my exam years at school.

Once, in a strange country where the window blinds were outside the buildings, I slept in a dark flat into the afternoon, until I heard a radio next door. I charged round to ask what they thought they were up to in the middle of the night, but in the street people were riding bicycles, whistling as they waited for the lights to change. The city was awake and eating lunch. I hopped back, a barefoot, crazy foreigner, and discovered the handle which opened the shutters. They pulled up with a rattling noise on the other side of the glass, opened like a great laughing mouth that had fooled me with its trick of darkness.

Not that my father ever played tricks. It just felt like that sometimes. Once he ordered a table and chairs. When they arrived my mother told the delivery man that there must have been a mistake and made him take them back to the warehouse. My father had to pay twice to have them delivered.

'But what do we need a table and chairs for?' she kept repeating. 'There's hardly room to move as it is.'

And then he took us off to Todmorden. He'd booked up at a farmhouse. Mother hadn't a clue. She thought she was going to see her sister in Wales. All the way on the train she kept looking out of the window.

'I'm sure we're going the wrong way.'

That night she had to call her sister who sneezed repeatedly and said she'd caught her death standing out in the rain all day at Llanelli station.

Holidays usually didn't figure that prominently. Instead we punctuated the year with church festivals. My mother's task one Easter was to decorate the parlour. Everything had to be perfect for the resurrection.

'If Christ can rise from the dead for us, the least I can do is that front room,' she said as she pored over paintcharts in Woolworths.

She held out swatches of colour match and wallpaper towards me. I was supposed to be the artistic one.

'Well what do you think?' she'd say. 'Can you put these two colours together at all?' and her eyes would be a blaze of lemon yellow.

But overnight we heard banging and crashing.

'Are we being burgled or what?' And her hand must have slid over to his half of the bed, which was empty.

All the landing lights were on. My eldest brother, rubbing his eyes and half blinded was sent in front.

'They've got your father,' she whispered, crouching behind her son as we crept down the stairs in trembling procession.

The parlour door was ajar.

'Oh, Good-God-Almighty-Sammy!' she said. My father stood there in a pair of overalls.

'Go on all of ye, back to your beds. I'm just getting the ceiling done.' He clapped his hands to shoo us out. 'It will be ready in the morning. It's a surprise. You can't see it until it's finished.'

She stared at him.

'But I was still choosing the paint. I haven't decided on the colour scheme yet.'

'Ah,' he said, touching the side of his nose. 'I have my ways.'

That night I couldn't sleep. The lights never went off on the landing. I lay in bed for hours listening, and thought I could hear sobbing from her room.

He must have worked like a maniac all night. It was a good thing

Those Sailing Ships of His Boyhood Dreams

the next day was Saturday. I noticed that the parlour door was locked.

He had the key in his waistcoat pocket as he sat down to breakfast with a tired, but triumphant smile.

'Well?' he said at last. 'Aren't you going to ask me?'

My mother looked out of the kitchen window to where, in the yard, a bike rusted. Her eyes were red and she ate nothing. She wouldn't sit down at the table with us but stood on her own drinking tea by the sink.

He clapped his hands. 'The Grand Unveiling Ceremony.'

We trooped in behind him. The smell of paint would have knocked you over.

I looked around. The wallpaper was sage green and it reminded me of the mould that grows on certain types of cheese. All around the skirting board the new paint had spattered the lino. It was slapdash and hadn't been allowed to dry properly between coats. Brush hairs clung to the gloss and on the window side the new green paper had dark brown marks where his paint-smeared hand must have touched for balance.

The *pièce de résistance* was over the fireplace. Two huge ships with masts bent their sails into the wind and swept the foamy sea of the picture wallpaper.

My mother was silent.

'Well?' he said.

My younger brother thought it was great, but Brendan just went over to Mam and touched her hair ever so gently.

'Well what do you think?' my father asked again.

'It looks like a chip shop,' she said at last and Brendan started to laugh.

'Shall we get some pink dragons?' he giggled. 'We could open up as a Chinese take-away. What do you say Mam?'

But she didn't say anything. She walked out of the room leaving us marooned, watching the cut and swell of water as if the last fleet had sailed, and we had missed it.

She didn't set foot in the parlour for almost a year until my dad gave in and emulsioned over the lot in time for Lent. The ships gave in finally to floral stripes, then to lozenges of pattern, to layers of paint and woodchip, as they sunk deeper beneath the new.

Those Sailing Ships of His Boyhood Dreams

I had moved away and my father was long dead, when one day I happened to walk past a model ship in Holborn. A kit in the window caught my eye. On the box was a picture of an enormous galleon that must have sailed right off the original wallpaper.

I didn't go in and buy it to sit up all night recapturing my childhood with slivers of balsa wood and glue. At the time it felt as though it had just caught my eye. I don't believe that I slowed my steps. Neither did I go back to the shop at a later date to stare at the picture from the pavement. I noticed it and am sure that I kept walking, to wherever I had to go and I forget now, what pressing appointment I had to keep. And I can't have forgotten those ships, when a single one glimpsed again on a cardboard box brings the room back to me.

But memory is a wayward beast. I want to recall my mother's sadness, instead I keep thinking how my father had no history. Not like my friend's dad who fancied he was James Dean. There were no photos of my father. He had no wayward youth, no leather-jacketed memories of once when he was wild. Always an adult, even in his tales of childhood he was a small version of a man. And it seems right that if only for a year, between the time of celebration and the time of fasting, he had the *Boys' Own* bedroom he always wanted.

That night after I'd noticed the box in the window, my sleep was full of those sailing ships of my father's boyhood dreams.